Fifty Shades Of Hood Love

Kia Jones

Fifty Shades Of Hood Love

Copyright © 2022 by Kia Jones

All rights reserved.

Published in the United States of America.

All rights reserved. No part of this publication may be reproduced, distributed, or transmitted in any form or by any means, including photocopying, recording, or other electronic or mechanical methods, without the prior written permission of the publisher, except in the case of brief quotations embodied in critical reviews and certain other noncommercial uses permitted by copyright law. For permission requests, please contact: www.colehartsignature.com

This is a work of fiction. Names, characters, places, and incidents either are the products of the author's imagination or are used fictitiously. Any resemblance of actual persons, living or dead, businesses, companies, events, or locales is entirely coincidental. The publisher does not have any control and does not assume any responsibility for author or third-party websites or their content.

The unauthorized reproduction or distribution of this copyrighted work is a crime punishable by law. No part of the book may be scanned, uploaded to or downloaded from file sharing sites, or distributed in any other way via the Internet or any other means, electronic, or print, without the publisher's permission. Criminal copyright infringement, including infringement without monetary gain, is investigated by the FBI and is punishable by up to five years in federal prison and a fine of $250,000 (www.fbi.gov/ipr/).

This book is licensed for your personal enjoyment only. Thank you for respecting the author's work.

Published by Cole Hart Signature, LLC.

Mailing List

To stay up to date on new releases, plus get information on contests, sneak peeks, and more,

Go To The Website Below...

www.colehartsignature.com

Spin

Solved By Homicide

I cringed as Fray pretended to check Sway for weapons. His hands stopped every time he got to her juicy bottom and squeezed. He snatched her up and tossed her against the wall, right next to me. "I know you got something," he said as he fondled her perky breasts.

"She don't have anything, Fray. Give us a break."

"Shut up, Spin," he said, steadily harassing my friend.

Spin wasn't my name, by the way. It's kinda Spindarella. People know how I got my name. Just read it: Spin-da-rella. It's self-explanatory, but for anyone that's slow or just doesn't listen to drill music, I whack shit. I spin the block harder than niggas.

Streets had been calling me Spin for so long that they thought it was a government name.

My mom was a childish, fairytale wanna-be, soft ass bitch, so she named me Cinderella after her favorite movie. Cinderella Gipson, but as I got older and developed my own sense of style and voice, I spun that shit to Spindarella but Spin for short. Our crew was called the Spindarellas. Not because of my name but because we were some lethal baddies.

One might see my name and think I'm a dike, but I'm not. In fact, people told me all the time I should've been part of the modeling scene instead of the drill scene but fuck that. Models didn't have the money and power, and that's what I wanted. My city loved me, and they chanted my name everywhere I went. The DJs loved me. I wasn't a rapper, but that didn't stop them from yelling my name over the mic soon as I stepped in. Me and my crew were stepping on everything moving, and we were all bitches.

Though it was only about a dozen of us, we were heavy. We toted big guns and pistols too. We used to be the target for robberies and other petty things men tried to do to shut us down, but all that stopped once bodies started turning up on the bridges, hanging by the neck. On some real cartel shit.

When we first started the Spindarellas, it was just me and my best-friends Sway, Asha, and Tweety. Just like me, Sway was beautiful and, according to the city, *too pretty to be drilling*. We heard it all the time and didn't care.

Nobody could fuck with us. Well... today, that statement proved to be a bit false.

I stood with my chest against the wall and hands behind my back as I watched Sway on her stomach being illegally searched by Fray. Fray was her probation officer. I hated him but not more than Sway. She had good reason to feel how she felt.

"I don't have anything," she said.

I was the more sensitive one but sneakier too. Sway? She was easily angered and loud about it. I would weep about it, leaving any hood bitch to call me weak. Then, that same person would end up dead, and nobody knew it was me because I was so *weak*.

Sway stood 5'1 with light skin and the perfect Coke bottle shape. Unlike me, Sway didn't have any tattoos at all. Her skin was so smooth and perfect. What she did have were piercings. She had a tongue ring, nose rings on each side, and the top of her plump lips pierced. Sad to say, Sway was used to being fondled and seen as a sex symbol. In fact, she used it for her own personal gain, except for right now. She truly hated Fray. Mainly because he could do whatever he wanted to her, and she couldn't do anything to him. She kept trying to get assigned a new officer, but it never happened.

Fray looked over at me and back to Sway. He bit his bottom lip, not trying to hide his hard dick. "I have a dirty urine sample in my car with your name written on it," he told her.

It was early in the morning, and he was over there fucking with Sway. I swear I hated myself. We couldn't whack this nigga, and he was the one we needed dead the most. Judges heard rumors, of course—everyone did. So, she already told Sway if another probation officer is *mysteriously murdered*, the FBI would be brought in. Yeah, Sway was fucked, in all meanings of the word.

"Please, Fray, don't do this right now. Please, I'm begging you," Sway said, pleading with her eyes also.

"Fray, you know that sample ain't hers. You ain't even checked her this month."

"The police department don't know that. They damn sure ain't gon' believe two wannabe porn stars and drug lords."

"We're not porn stars," I said.

He snatched Sway, who was still handcuffed and pushed her toward the couch. "She's one today," he said as he bent Sway over the couch and snatched her panties off.

"Please," Sway whimpered. "Please don't do this."

He snatched the condom wrapper off and slid the condom on his deformed dick. Before he could slam into her, I squeezed my eyes shut and turned away.

The sound of his pelvis slapping against Sway's ass hurt me to my soul. Her cries and screams hit different this time. Fray had done this to her many times before, but this time was more hurtful to us because she'd just had a miscarriage a little over a week ago, and Fray knew that.

"Yeah, keep crying. You know that shit turns me on," he said as I heard him slap her ass.

My eyes were still closed, so I couldn't see—only hear. But

when I heard Sway gagging, I knew he was about to cum and making her swallow it all.

I heard him zip his pants. He then removed my cuffs and slowly walked to the front door. "Congratulations on passing yet another drug test. I'll come by next week for another." He winked at us and closed the door.

I quickly ran over to hug Sway, but she pushed me away. She sat on our cream colored couch with the stench of Fray's cheap cologne lingering on her. "I'm so sorry," I said as I fell to her feet and wrapped my arms around her legs. "I'm so sorry, Sway. I'm so fucking sorry. I love you so much."

She stood and walked away from me.

Sway and I were the hardest bitches in Dallas, and even we had problems that couldn't be solved by homicide.

My brother would be so disappointed in me right now.

I guess all fairytales ain't real. Not in the hood, no way.

SWAY
NO MERCY FOR MONSTERS

After cleaning up, I gave myself time to get right and got right back to the business.

Fray was a monster, but so was I. No mercy for monsters, so I didn't show much for myself. I looked at it as karma. With all the fucked up stuff I had done in the streets and was still doing, I was due for some karma. I just ain't think it would come this hard.

After showering, I sat on the toilet and put a thick pad in the seat of my panties. The bleeding had stopped but not completely. Fray had worsened it, but hopefully, it was only temporary.

After dressing, I stood in my full-length mirror, gazing at a picture of my fallen soldier, Houston. He was my bestie, Spin's, brother. They killed him last month in a drive-by. The messed up part about Houston was that he wasn't even in the streets like us. Yeah, he did his diddy with the drugs, but he wasn't doing no heavy sliding. That was all us, most of the time—the Spindarellas. My love just got caught in the crossfire. Then, on the day of the funeral, I found out I was pregnant. A little over a week ago, on my birthday, I had a miscarriage. I just felt like, damn, I couldn't win for losing.

We were at war, but it was necessary. We didn't start this; the opposition did. It started with one body years ago, and now bodies had piled up. Wasn't no copping deuces. We tried that and called a meeting. What do they do? They shot up the meeting spot and killed another friend of ours. So, fuck it, this was where we were at now.

The bad part in all of this was that we were beefing with niggas. Some grown ass, supposed to be gangstas, were beefing with women. Their reasons were because *the streets wasn't no place for bitches.* That's what Terry said. Terry was the head dude in charge of SAD boys. Slimy Affiliated Demons is what SAD boys stood for. They operated out of Ft Worth and Arlington, mostly in the Tarrant County area. It was a lot of them. We were so outnumbered by them that it made no sense.

They were behind the shooting that killed my love, my baby daddy, my future. He was my everything, and they did that. Now I couldn't rest until I took someone Terry loved deeply, and it was none other than that pit bull of his. I know it sounded stupid, but that clown loved nothing in the world more than that dog. He protected it like it worked for the president. He was the type to share a noodle with his dog and eat it all the way to the middle. He would kiss his dog and all type of shit. To be real, I wouldn't put it past him if he was fucking that damn dog. Diamond was the dog's name.

"We're running low on work. I'm going to see the plug today," Spin said as she grabbed the keys to her jeep. Seemed like we both got dressed at the same time.

Spin was a little shorter than me. She stood maybe five feet even. She was so hard on herself, but I understood why. She had a horrible, horrible childhood. The only thing that saved her from the evil going on in her house was her brother being released from juvenile at the tender age of sixteen. Had it not been for him, her white stepfather would've kept pouring bleach on her skin and making her wear blonde wigs.

Spin was a red bone and a little chubby. Her stomach had a little extra for a nigga to grab, but it wasn't outrageous. She didn't have hips, a juicy ass, and boobs like mine, but she was working with something. Her apple bottom was perfect for her small boobs and chubby stomach. It never stopped her from getting no nigga. She wore her hair in forty-inch red lace fronts, and I wore mine in my naturally long, blonde locs that came to the middle of my back. We were alike in so many ways, yet so different. Our differences were what made us get along so well.

I locked up since I was the last to leave our loft and hopped in my pink jeep.

As I passed the store, I saw Mama Crystal standing there waving her hands and running toward the street. I rolled my eyes and pulled over to the curb. "Here! Stop doing that shit every time you see me," I said as I tossed her a twenty-dollar bill. "And where did you get this blue wig? From a toy store?" I asked, chinking her another dub.

"I was gon' say, if you don't like it, change it." She flashed the money I'd just given her.

"Clown." I shook my head and blew her a kiss. "Go home!" I yelled as I drove off.

When I got to the red light, I pulled next to Spin and let the window down. She saw me and took her shades off. "Yo?"

"Can you toss me my Chanel frames, please? I sure been looking for them."

She laughed and tossed them. They landed on my lap. "I would've bought some more."

"I like these," I assured her.

"So, give me my green Chanel bag," she said, but the light turned green.

I sped off as we tossed each other the middle finger.

I went to the graveyard and laid down some roses on my love's tombstone, and headed to the trap on the north side. The north side wasn't our territory, but they didn't give us any trouble on the block we held down. At first, they gave us no trouble, but last night was the second time we got robbed in six months over there, so I needed to lay down some law.

Once there, I only noticed a yellow Camaro. That meant Tweety was on the spot alone. See, that was one problem right there. I snatched my shades off and hopped down from the jeep. Leaving it running, I paid a junkie to make sure nobody fucked with it.

I banged on the loud screen door. After a few minutes, she opened the door with her hair all over her head and yawned. I pushed past her with an attitude. "I can smell the liquor on your breath. You was in the spot alone and drunk?"

Tweety chugged down the rest of what was left in a beer can. Only Tweety could make drinking beer look like a Coca-Cola commercial. I saw a bruise under her hazel eye. She was high yellow, so it was hard to hide bruises. "You're the one who fired all the workers, and now you got me babysitting traps. You know this ain't my shit. This what Rel and 'em supposed to be doing, not me."

"Rel on suspension from working the spots. She acts too careless with the front door."

Tweety plopped on the couch. "Well, what she in the crew for? She ain't out here dropping bodies. She can't work the traps. What do we have her for? Because we all grew up together? That answer ain't working for me no more." She looked exhausted, and I truly understood.

Tweety, just like Spin and me, was one of the top killers in our click. The others were down to ride too, but they were only really good at fighting. They were squeamish when it came to blood and dead bodies.

"You right. I'm going to talk to her today and let her know if she can't hold her weight, then she isn't needed."

Tweety agreed by giving me a thumbs up. She was the one with a nonchalant personality. Wasn't too much she cared about. Oh, and good luck getting a reaction out of her. "We need tissue in here. It's like two rolls left."

"How hard the trap roll last night?"

"Harder than a mothafucka."

"What happened to your eye?" I asked directly after. I knew how to catch her off guard.

"I have no idea. I was drunk a few days ago and woke up like this. I think I fell."

"Damn."

I believed her. Tweety was a stone cold, high-functioning alcoholic. We tried to get her help, but it never worked. It was so odd, but Tweety was actually at her best when she was intoxicated. When she was sober, we all knew because she annoyed the hell out of us. She wouldn't shut up, be still, or keep one train of thought.

"You didn't pass out while you were here alone, right?"

"Duh. I ain't crazy. I'll mix the crown with Red Bull before I crash at anybody's trap."

"Got the tapes?"

She nodded and turned on the TV.

When the spot got hit last night, Tweety came over to stay the night and keep guard. She wasn't supposed to be alone. That pissed me off so bad.

The footage from last night played as I sat down between Tweety's legs and handed her some grease from my purse, so she could grease my scalp for me. I loved her hands.

On the footage, I watched as Rel left the door unattended while going to the back to get some drugs. The dude at the door had on an all-white shirt.

"Watch this," Tweety said as if we were watching an entertaining movie.

The guy slid a mask on after the camera already saw his face and motioned across the dark street. That's when four men invaded the spot and pistol whipped Rel, dropping her to her knees and robbing the house.

Luckily, they didn't know that we never kept big shit in the open. It was hidden. All they got was a few ounces of coke and some heroin.

On their way out, I paused it. "You see that?" I asked Tweety.

"Yep."

"Hurry up with my hair. We're going to see Rel," I said as I turned the tv off. I had seen what I needed to see.

She didn't bust at them dudes because she knew one of them. It was her ex. One of the many men she had been dumb over. He was still robbing her dumbass not-so-blind.

SPIN
A BIG FORGIVENESS

I waited in the warehouse off Hampton Street for the delivery. I chose the west side because it was the safest for both parties to meet. West Dallas usually stayed neutral in any beef that went on in the city. They didn't really do or tolerate a lot of unnecessary drama. They were more of the get money type. I mean, we were too, but them west Dallas hustlers were different.

For years, before we were even born, it was understood that the west was off limits in most situations. A lot of them cats were older anyway. See, over in Oakcliff, the North, and other parts of the Dallas-Fort Worth metroplex, the youngsters had mostly taken over. We weren't trying to hear none of that 'OG, respect your elders' bullshit. We made them niggas respect the minors. We weren't minors, but we were younger than a lot of people at only twenty-three.

Water dropping and the sound of rats added to the darkness of the warehouse. I would say this was a terrible place to meet.

"You always smell so good," I heard a voice say. I turned around with my gun in hand and finger on the trigger. He tossed his hands up and smiled. "It's just me."

"Terry," I sighed and put my gun away. "You got what I asked for?" I pulled out the money I would owe from my bra.

"You still ain't talking to me?" He looked disappointed.

Terry stood at about an even six feet. His hair was in a high-top fade, but he sponged it, leaving it to look like little nappy snakes sticking up in his head. Instead of diamonds, he rocked golds. He did this purposely. He loved golds, and they looked so good on him.

"Do you have it?"

He dropped the bag in front of me. "So, you can't talk to me, but you can still score from me?" he asked as he walked closer to me with a childish grin.

"Until I find out who killed my brother, you have nothing to say to me."

"But I swear it wasn't me, baby. I told you that. You know I would've been told you that. Why would I shoot into a crowd my baby in? I would never hurt you."

"Yeah, whatever." I tried to give him the money.

He pushed it back. "It's on me." He tried to pull me in for an embrace, but I pushed him away. "You got me fucked up." He pulled me in anyway and held me, and boy, did it feel good. "I miss you."

"Who killed my brother?"

"I don't know, baby. You gotta know I'm on that."

"You don't even like my crew. You wouldn't kill for us."

"But I'll kill for you. Believe that."

I finally backed away. "I have to go before Sway figures out I'm here."

"How would she? We made sure of that, right?"

"Why you keep smiling?" I asked.

"Man, baby, I'm happy to see you. Goddamn, I can't be happy to see you?" He had his hands out and palms up.

"Goofy."

"You know you miss me." He pushed up on me and picked me up.

I didn't fight him. "Ughhh, they gon' kill me," I said as I allowed him to kiss my neck.

"Ain't nobody gon' fuck with you," he said in a more serious tone. He then went back to kissing me. "Baby, can I have some pussy? Pleaaassse?" He playfully whined like a child.

"No."

"Please? I haven't fucked since the last time you and I had sex. I'm saving myself for you."

We shared a laugh. I could never stay mad at him, but I had to at least try to stand on Spindarella business.

"No. Get off me."

He gently put me down. "I ain't gon' force you."

"Thanks." I grabbed the bag and tossed it over my shoulders.

He watched me over his shoulder as I walked out. "Know you want to give that pussy up."

"Bye, see you next time." I chunked up the deuce.

Once I got in the jeep, he called my phone. "What, Terry?"

"That's how you do me? Run off with my heart and drugs? All free of charge?"

"I tried to pay," I said as I watched him emerge from the darkness of the warehouse, coming into the light.

He wasn't all the way out but far enough to where I could see him. He leaned his sexy, tall, and lanky body against the frame of the raggedy door.

"Look at me," he said.

I looked up at him and turned the car off. "Why you always do this to me?" I leaned back in my seat. "You know what you do to me."

"Baby, I swear on Earth I ain't have nothing, and I mean nothing, to do with the death of your brother." Earth was one of his homies that was murdered, and everyone blamed it on our crew. But in all honesty, we didn't have anything to do with it. "I believed you when you told me y'all ain't do that to Earth. And what I do? Baby, I stood down and made everyone else stand down too."

SAD boys had outnumbered us something vicious. They could've been wiped us out but hadn't done it. Spindarellas thought it was because they couldn't outsmart us, when in reality, they were letting us make it, purposely. Every once in a while, shit was out of my control because Sway was trigger happy. When she did some crazy shit, it was nothing Terry could do because all is fair in love and war. I understood that. I couldn't help who I loved, and I loved him.

"I have to find who did it."

"And I'll help you. But only for you, not for Sway. Only because he was your brother, not because it was her nigga."

"I respect your honesty."

"Then come here. Let me tell you something."

I sighed and shook my head because I knew in less than five minutes, I would have his thick dick inside of me. And I would love it. He stepped back into the darkness and hung up the phone.

I walked in behind him and closed the heavy door, locking it. We went into a vacant office right in the corner of the warehouse. Terry undid his pants and picked me up, gently placing me on the old desk. He kissed me so softly as he slid inside of me. Once he got deep in, he pulled both of my thighs toward him to make us even closer.

As he grabbed my ass cheeks and made love to me, I tossed my head back. "Fuuuuck," he said under his breath. I held on to him tightly like I never wanted to let go. I guess because—shit, I didn't want to let him go. "I love you so much, bruh," he said between kisses.

"I love you, too."

"You belong to me. You my baby. You know that?" He stroked me harder but slower.

I nodded. "I know."

The crew didn't know, but SAD boys didn't have any real beef with us. It started months back when someone shot and killed one of ours. In retaliation, we did the same to one of them. Only to find out they really ain't do nothing to us. But, by then, the bodies had already started piling up.

Terry let us slide a few times because we were women, but Sway kept doing the most, so he gave his crew the okay to start sniping back. He told her the streets wasn't for her if she was mad at men for shooting back at bitches.

I met Terry right before the bodies started dropping while in Ft Worth one day, visiting my mother in a nursing home. Though Bell Marie wasn't that old, years and years of drug and alcohol abuse had taken a toll on her mental. She couldn't remember shit. She barely remembered me, but she definitely remembered my brother. In her mind, he was still alive.

Terry was at the same nursing home, visiting his grandmother. He saw me coming out of Bell Marie's room and stopped me right then. Said he had to get me, and we'd been on since then.

When the beef started, he made a promise to not let it come between us, but I had to promise the same thing. So, I promised, but I needed to find out who killed my brother before Sway put a rift between Terry and me that couldn't be repaired.

When we were done, I pulled my hoochie mama shorts over my ass and watched as he got dressed. "When you get a bulletproof vest?" I asked.

He laughed. "Shid, when Sway lost her damn mind."

I frowned. "I'm sorry. All I need to need is to find out who did it, and I promise I'll make her stop."

"I hope so. I ain't gon' even front wit'cha, baby, I ain't got a lot of patience left in me for them clumsy ass Spindarellas. Them hoes starting to annoy me."

"Hey," I said and pushed his shoulder.

"What? I'm serious. I got so much shit going on. Ain't got time to be fooling around with nobody steppin' for nothing. Especially no entitled bitches." I knew that was aimed at Sway. He couldn't stand her.

"I'm one of them."

"I know, but one of them bullets she sent last week almost hit one of us."

"She had a miscarriage. I'm sorry."

"Fuck her and that dead ass baby. She sends another one, and I'ma send a few back. If I can make my niggas stand down, what's the hold up with you making your bitches stand down? You ain't got no rank?"

"I do, but—you know what? You're right. I'll try to talk to them today."

"That's all I'm asking. You ain't gotta tell them you love me. I know you love me. We know you love me. The world ain't got to know, but see if you can get a handle on this shit before I unleash them boys. And when I do that, the only person I'm marking off limits is you. Them other bitches' ass is grass."

"Okay, baby."

"Give me some love." He leaned down for a kiss, and I kissed him back. "I'm out. I love you."

"I love you more," I said as he left through the front door.

This was about to be like moving a mountain, but I had to try. He was right. For far too long, he let my crew make it on the strength of me. The least I could do was try to talk them down.

SWAY
SHOULD'VE DUCKED

I paced the floor, trying to keep from digging into Rel's ass. She really sat there and tried to convince me that the dude on the camera wasn't her ex.

Tweety laughed. "Do you know that we see this footage? Just like you?"

"Duh, Tweety. I know that." Rel stood up and made sure the front door to her apartment was locked.

Rel was taller than the rest of us, standing at 5'11. She looked like Naomi Campbell, but that's because she wanted to. No, she literally got some cosmetic work done to look like Naomi Campbell.

"So, what should we do with him? Huh, Rel?" I asked, studying her face really hard to see any sign of weakness.

She walked to the kitchen and pulled out a pan from the oven. "I made bacon."

I looked at Tweety and dropped into the love seat. So desperately, I tried to contain my anger. "Listen, eat your bacon. Do your thing, and I will wait. We going on a drill."

She looked like she wanted to cry. "What?"

"And no, you're not going to just pay back what he stole. This nigga so embarrassed to be fucking with you that he robs you blind every chance he gets. What if one day he comes with someone and can't control that person? What if he comes with some niggas that decide to kill you one day? Fuck that, keep the money," I said. "We sending a message today."

Tweety nodded. "We getting Just, Dalvin, and Laytron," she said.

Laytron was Rel's ex, and the other two were his close friends. Every time Rel was robbed, those three were always the common denominators. They had no respect for us. They robbed the trap anytime Rel was there alone. It's like they knew we would whack them, but maybe Laytron felt like we wouldn't because of Rel. That pissed me off even more.

"Do we have to do Laytron?" Rel put her head down.

"Why shouldn't we?"

"He loves me. He really does. You know what it is with him. He don't want people to know he gets down like that," Rel said.

"Like what?" I asked.

She looked down at herself. "You know, with me being born a guy and all."

"A lot of people don't even know you're a guy," Tweety said.

"But enough people know. And Laytron is just keeping up appearances. He didn't mean any harm."

"So, you mean to tell me, out of all the people to rob in the city, he can only rob you? Shut the fuck up and get dressed," I said as I snatched my bag and headed to the jeep.

On my way out, I snatched her phone, so she wouldn't get any bright ideas and call to warn him. She did that, and I would put a bullet in her ass.

As I walked down the stairs to my whip, a group of dudes approached me from the side. I hadn't seen them before, but I didn't like how close they were to me, so I made sure my hand was inside my purse, on the tool.

"Damn, you fine as hell. This all you?" one dude asked as he held my door open for me, but instead of letting me get inside, he got in. "Oooohhwwwe. I'll look good in this bitch." He looked at the steering wheel and then back at me. "Where the keys?"

Grabbing the bridge of my nose, I chuckled. "Get out of my car, dude."

"Or what?" a female asked, coming from the back of the crowd. She had her hair braided and hands on her lil' rusty gun.

See, this was my type of shit. I loved to show a nigga or bitch that I would always be the one who gave one less fuck.

Tweety came down the stairs with Rel right behind her. The group of flunkies didn't pay them any mind. If so, they would've seen two guns pointed at them all from the stairs.

"I don't have time for this. Move." I yanked dude out of the car, and he swung on me.

As I fell back, I saw the crowd rushing toward me.

Bow! Bow! Bow!

I let the first three shots ring from inside my purse. Tweety shot at them as they ran away, and Rel ran over to make sure I was okay. "I'm good," I said, allowing her to help me up.

"Got one," Tweety said as she walked near the parking lot and saw a splash of blood. "I think it was the girl with the gun."

"It was the dude who pushed me," I corrected as I dusted myself off. "He was the last to run. He got him in the foot."

She shrugged. "If he ain't know, now he knows not to fuck with us. Somebody should've warned him." Tweety hopped in the front passenger side while Rel got in the back seat, still quiet.

I checked myself in the mirror to see if the scrape on my elbow looked as bad as it felt.

"Oh, I'm good," I said when I saw it was a little scratch.

"Where he be at?" I asked.

"Who?" Tweety answered.

I looked back at Rel. "I ain't fucking around. Where the nigga be at?"

"He be in the West, but I really don't think we should go fucking around over there. They hold a neutral ground on everything, and we don't want to lose that grounding," Tweety said. Her drunk self be on point sometimes.

"You right." I tossed Rel her phone. "Call him and tell him to meet up tonight. Tell him to meet you in a spot like behind Fuel city."

"He ain't gon' do it."

"You know how to make that nigga agree. Tell him you want to suck his dick or something."

She smacked her lips. The fact that she was actually a he fucked me up about Rel because she was soft as hell. What type of human lets another human rob them all the time? And especially when the other human is supposed to love them.

"Hey, Laytron..." she started spitting her game.

"We gon' have to do something about her sooner or later," Tweety whispered in my ear.

I nodded in agreement. "I'm already knowing."

After she got off the phone, she said, "You don't think we should wait a little while longer?"

I turned the radio up and ignored her. As we rode on Highway 35, past Inwood, Tweety turned the radio down and pointed at the huge building, which was soon to be a strip club. "They said it's the hottest club the city has seen in years, and the grand opening is in two days. So how the hell would they know?" she said.

"What's it called?" I wanted to know.

Rel leaned forward. "I think it's called Fetish or something of that nature."

"Obsessed!" Tweety proclaimed like she was excited to have remembered the name.

"The owner is some big shot from Indiana, but I heard he's Jamaican. Who knows?" Tweety said, drinking a beer.

"Tweety, you're the only bitch I know that wake up drinking beer. Or wake up drinking at all."

She looked at me and shrugged. "Ain't no use complaining about it every time you see me drink. I been like this."

"But that don't mean you can't change," Rel said.

"And you shut the fuck up. Don't make me get on your ass," I said as I fixed the mirror so I could focus on her in the back seat.

A bright idea then passed through my mind, causing me to smile. After we shot Laytron, I would toss his body in front of the biggest attraction the city has ever seen and send the picture to a Tea page on social media. Club Obsessed was about to get more attention. He could thank me later, whoever he was.

When we got back to Oakcliff, I stopped at Rudy's Chicken and parked while I ordered all of us some food. The line was long, as always, so while we waited, I let the window down and tossed my leg through the opened space.

"Put that leg down before I bite it," Hercules said as he snuck up on me.

I laughed. Hercules was a big, tall, fat nigga who could fight his ass off. Put him in the ring, one on one with anyone, and I bet they'd fold. The hood always held boxing matches with different people. Hercules never took a loss. It was to the point that if they put him against anyone, he automatically won. Either that person was a no-show, or they tapped out five minutes into the first round. It was wild.

A few of the Spindarellas would join and fight, but most girls in the hood were scared to fight us in fear that if they won, we'd drill them. So, most of the time, we just went to watch and bullshit.

"You guys, I'm serious. Do we have to do this tonight? I can't just get fucked one more time?"

Tweety gave Rel a blank stare and looked over at me. "Don't look over here. You better tell her, because if I do, I'ma hurt her feelings." This weak in the knees thing was starting to piss me off. "Find another nigga," is all I said. My mind was made. "We let him slide before, and we don't even do things like that."

"Na, for real," Tweety agreed. "Then I heard you ain't the only tranny he's sticking it to." Tweety discreetly nudged me, so I could watch Rel's reaction. She was losing it back there and trying to act like she wasn't. Her eyes watered as she shook her head and folded her arms.

"Fuck 'em," Rel said.

"I heard it's that lady y'all called Mama Madison," I added.

The thing is, we weren't joking at all. In fact, we were very serious. We just wanted Rel to open her stupid eyes.

Laytron was known to dick down punks on the low. Everyone knew it. He would brag about how he used them for money and how they would do anything for him. Maybe he was right because look how he had my girl.

"Don't go out sad, Rel. Fuck that nigga. After we drill him, I'll take you out to a bar," Tweety said.

I laughed. "You always taking someone to a bar. Bitch, take her to eat or something."

"Bars have food."

"You know what I meant."

"I'll check on the food," Rel said and got out with her head down.

"I feel so bad for her. Ain't no more niggas to fuck with besides Laytron?" Tweety wanted to know.

"Yeah, but you know she don't like openly gay niggas. She likes them trap house banging, downlow ass niggas."

"She wants a nigga to thug her so bad."

"Facts," I said.

As we listened to slow jams on 105.7 and enjoyed the hot summer breeze, we heard a small commotion. And then it got louder, which caused Tweety and I to grab our heat and turn back. It was Rel and Mama Madison arguing. Standing behind Mama Madison's big ass was Laytron.

"Out of all days, he chose today," I said as we put the guns up and grabbed our brass knuckles and tasers.

Mama Madison was a well-loved punk in her middle thirties who was known to take down low men from young punks that she called her *children*. I never understood why Rel even trusted her.

"Ain't nobody rob you. Man, Madison, whoop this bitch," Laytron said as he stepped to the side.

Mama Madison had some huge implanted breasts with a deformed ass, thanks to ass shots that she did herself. She wore her hair in the latest hairstyles, but today, it was wrapped in a head rag.

She had her long nails in Rel's face. "You heard what he said. It's over. Now get!" All of Mama Madison's *children* gathered behind her, thinking they were all about to jump Rel.

Poor Rel didn't look like she wanted to fight. Seemed like she ain't even have no fight left in her. She was hurt. This made me want to drill Laytron even harder. I was going to make him suffer. He stood his light skinned, pimple-faced self to the side as Mama Madison and company ganged up on my friend.

When Tweety and I stepped on the pavement, all eyes were on us. They already knew what we were about, so the ones who knew better started backing away. Wasn't no telling if we were having fun or guns. The only way to be safe was to stay out of our way completely.

I shot a deadly glance over at Laytron. "It's not enough you rob her blind, but you want to embarrass her?" I pointed at Mama Madison. "For this big body ass bitch?"

When I said that, all hell broke loose. Several punks held Mama Madison back. Her purse dropped to the ground, and Laytron hurriedly grabbed it and ran the other way.

"Such a bum," Tweety said, her eyes following Laytron all the way to the train tracks.

Meanwhile, Mama Madison was just about to close in on Rel. I was over it. I turned around and grabbed our food with the sack that had my name. I then told Rel and Tweety to back up. Once my girls were in the clear, I pulled out my pepper spray and maced everyone in the crowd. I had the good pepper spray that had distance and width to it. Everyone in front of me was coughing and yelling about how much it burned.

I walked back to the jeep and hopped inside. "The whole

crowd, though?" Tweety laughed. "I saw some elderly citizens in there."

I placed my arm on the back of her seat and backed away. "Should've ducked." My eyes traveled to a distraught Rel. She hyperventilated as she let a stream of tears fall onto my pink seats. "Everything will be okay. I promise you," I said with the plans I had for him on my mind.

"Yeah, next time, he will think twice before using someone," Tweety said.

"Think twice?" I asked. "Girl, he ain't about to be thinking *at all*." That was a fact. He was disgusting and pitiful, making Rel look pitiful right alongside his dusty self.

"How could Mama Madison do this to me?"

Tweety climbed over my seat, so she could be in the back, consoling an overly dramatic Rel. Shaking my head, I took a few salty fries from the bag and stuffed them in my mouth. All that soft shit was irritating, especially over a bum who literally just ran off with someone's purse. That was some low-level, petty crime shit that the cops didn't even touch. It was weak.

As I drove toward the loft to collect the drugs from Spin, I seriously contemplated what to do with Rel. The stuff she was doing was truly unacceptable. I believed she was hurt, and I understood that, but to let this coward rob you more than once? It's not like all the drugs belonged to her. On top of that, it was already tough gaining respect out in these streets as women hustlers. We didn't need her to make these niggas feel like robbing us was like taking candy from a baby. She needed to be reprimanded. That was that. The more I looked at her through the rearview, the more upset I got.

The entire way to the loft, she cried. Her real voice even broke through a bit; that's how hard she cried.

After parking, I turned back and said, "Is it that serious? You doing too much." She wiped her tears and got out of the jeep without responding. "I'm just saying, I've been through worse in a day, and you don't see me crying. Spin, Tweety, Asha, shid, most of us been through worse shit than a nigga playing with us."

"Give her a break," Tweety said as she grabbed the food from me and ate some fries on the way inside.

Once inside, Rel poured a glass of cognac for her and Tweety. Just a couple of shots. Spin came around the corner and tossed a backpack on the countertop. "Why you looking so ugly?" she asked Rel.

Tweety and I laughed. I grabbed some paper plates and put all of us some food on them. "Laytron robbed her again, then she caught him at Rudy's with Mama Madison," I said as I handed Spin her plate.

"Ouch. Your friend Mama Madison?" she asked Rel.

"She's not my friend."

"We been telling your big goofy ass that's not your friend," I said. "We your friends. Just because she takes dick in the ass too don't mean she relates more. We all been oppressed before."

Tweety had something on her mind. I could tell by the way she divided her attention between Rel and me. "What's wrong?" I wanted to know.

"I'll just say it. Rel, you're becoming a liability."

"Says the woman who's literally drunk all day every day," Rel snapped back, sitting on the floor.

"Yeah, but I'm always on point. I ain't ever let no nigga rob me. Especially not nigga I been fucking on. You crazy."

"I didn't know it was him."

"You looked right at him!" Tweety screamed, and she never did that. She was upset.

The two began to bicker. As they spit boxed, I watched Spin carefully. She didn't eat much of anything. The fries were held on her tongue, but she didn't intake any of them. Finally done with trying, she dropped the fries and drank from her Sprite.

"What's good? You a'ight?" I asked.

"I think we should reconsider the ongoing beef with SAD

boys." When she said that, Tweety and Rel both hushed and looked at her like she was crazy.

"And why is that?" I asked.

"Are we really sure they did this? I mean, how do we even know?"

"Streets talked," Tweety said. I remained silent. She had lost her rabbit mind. Everyone was going crazy.

"Yeah, but did they really? Some junkies told us them boys did it, but junkies are not to be trusted. SAD boys all in Ft. Worth, so we don't really know."

"Who do you suppose did it?" I asked.

She shrugged. "We can find out. We ain't the only bitches trying to get respect out here. We've made so many enemies, we can't just say Terry and 'em killed my brother."

"So, what? You want us to stand down? Or what we even talking about?" Tweety asked.

"Ain't no standing down," I snapped.

Spin snapped her head toward me, peeping my tone. "You know what, Sway? You get on my fuckin' nerves thinking you run shit. When it comes to shit like war in the streets, we are supposed to take polls, and the majority wins. Not we just all do what *Sway* says."

"Relax, Spin," Rel said, looking nervous.

"No, I'm tired of her. She makes decisions for all of us, and it affects us. You too fucking trigger happy. We slide on opps! These days, you been sliding on any and everybody. You the reason we in a lot of shit because you have no understanding."

"Fuck I need understanding for in the streets?"

"Because bodies are piling up, Sway, and it's bringing unnecessary heat to us," Tweety said.

Rel nodded in agreement with them. "They're right, Sway. I think we should stand down and at least try to figure out who did it."

"We know who did it. Fuck is wrong with y'all?"

"How do we know that?" Spin asked.

"They're our sworn enemies. It's common sense."

"No, they're your sworn enemies. Sway, let's just keep it all the way one hunna. You shot at them niggas and got mad when they shot back," Spin said, now standing. "Every time they chill, you start it back up. What the hell is even up with you these days?"

Tweety and Rel just nodded in agreement. Fucking weaklings. "I ain't standing down."

"Nah, let's do a vote, and the majority wins. If everyone votes to stand down until we find who really did it, and you keep attacking them boys, you will be reprimanded. Rules are rules, and they apply to everyone," Tweety said.

"Including you," Spin added.

"Okay, bet. Get them bitches on the phone. Let's see," I said as I called Asha, putting her on speaker while everyone else called the others.

"I'm at work. What's up?"

"This early?"

"I had to do some new training before my shift tonight. What's up?"

"Asha, we're doing a vote. It ain't gon' take long. So, you think we should drill them niggas over in Ft. Worth or stand down until we are one hundred percent sure they did it? Even though we know they did it," I said.

"Who? SAD boys?" Asha asked.

"Yeah, them," I confirmed.

"I say stand down. We really don't know if they did it or not. Definitely stand down. That's my vote. Bye, my partner is walking back to the cop car," she said and quickly hung up.

I looked up to see everyone else on the phone but eavesdropping on Asha and me. Asha was the most levelheaded out of all of us, so when she said to stand down, I knew that was the only vote that mattered to them.

After everyone was called, the votes were in. They wanted us to stand down. Everyone chose to stand down. Not one person agreed to drill them. "Okay, so we stand down." I walked away.

This the type of stuff I be talking about.

With anger and force, I slammed the door to my room behind me.

SPIN
Public Display of Affection

Me, Sway, Tweety, and Rel laid low as she waited for the call to come through from Laytron. Little did he know, we were sitting on the apartments he and his boys trapped from. We paid Sway and 'em old foster mom, Mama Crystal, to use her car. Mama Crystal never used her old beat-up Honda, so she always let us use it. She was the only crackhead any of us really trusted. Meeting junkies who had great relationships with their children said something within itself. Every child Mama Crystal pushed from her twat or brought in as a foster kid loved the ground she walked on. They all tried to get her help, but year after year, she refused.

I turned my nose up and rolled the window down. "Ew, who farted?"

"Sorry," Rel said. "I'm nervous."

"The fact that drills still make you nervous irks my soul," Sway said, tracing her long nails around the steering wheel.

"Everything irks your soul," I said.

"You been having a lot to say to me today. What's up?" She looked over at me like she wanted to snatch me by my throat.

Sway and I fought the most, but that's because we loved each other the most and knew each other the longest. She met me at seven. Asha came into the picture when I was eight, and Tweety a few months after that. We all came up in the same projects, but Sway, Tweety, and Asha were all raised by the same foster mom, Mama Crystal, who lived next door to us at the time. Their foster mom brought them all in at different times, but she had Sway first. Which is why I met her first.

"You guys just drop it," Rel said. "I'm already nervous."

"Shut up, Rel!" Sway and I yelled back in unison.

My phone rang. When I saw it was my boo, I decided to answer. They didn't have to know who was on the phone. They weren't paying attention to me, no way.

"Hey, baby," I answered.

"You busy?"

"No."

"You with them bitches?"

I sighed. "Watch your mouth, and yes, I am."

"What happened with what we talked about?"

"Yeah," was all I could say without drawing suspicions from anyone in the car.

"So, they agreed to stand down?"

"Yes, baby. You have nothing to worry about."

"Bet. Can I see you tonight? Let's get a room downtown. A nice room."

"We just had sex."

"I want some more."

"Who's she talking to?" I heard Tweety ask Sway.

"The dude she be getting drugs from. Never met him, but he got some playa prices."

"What time?"

"I'm already at the room. I need to talk to you, too. It's really important."

"You trying to break up?" I jokingly asked.

"Hell nah. You know better than that. I just need to talk to you. I ain't want to tell you earlier because I had somewhere to be."

"Okay, when I'm finished doing what I'm doing, I'll be through."

"Bet."

We disconnected the phone.

Sway was in her phone playing a game while Tweety and Rel were literally breathing down my neck. "Who's that?" Tweety asked.

"My boo."

"Yeah, of course, but who's your boo?" Rel asked immediately after.

"Can y'all not?" I said, getting frustrated with the third degree.

"There goes the man of the hour," Sway said as Laytron came from around the corner.

He talked loudly on the phone while counting some money. He looked to be alone. Just as we all tossed on our masks, preparing to step out, a van pulled next to Laytron, and two masked assailants tossed him inside.

"You have got to be fucking kidding me," I said as I snatched the mask off and slammed my back against the seat.

"I know you fucking lying," Tweety said.

The only person who didn't seem to be upset was Rel. I didn't agree with a lot of things Sway did, but this was a drill I truly looked forward to. Laytron wasn't only messing over someone I cared about, but he also had some talk going around about us being soft. That was never good.

"Them Dracos in the trunk?" Sway asked.

I saw the wheels spinning in her head.

"Yeah," Tweety said.

"Sway, please, no," Rel said.

I rested my face in my palms. "You're about to snatch him from the van."

She sped out of the parking lot. "*We* are."

"This is what I mean when I said you have a problem,"

Tweety said. "Dude already just got snatched up. What we going after him for?" Tweety wanted to know.

She didn't answer. Instead, she burned rubber until we got to the end of the street. She then pulled right in front of them before they could leave the neighborhood. I stood in front of the van with my Draco pointed. Tweety stood in the back with her automatic. Rel and Sway stood right by the sliding door.

I noticed a face in the passenger seat making eye contact with me, so I used that chance to speak. "We just want Laytron."

On the driver's side, they slightly opened the window. Only enough to where we could hear them clearly. "This one is ours. I don't want to run y'all over. So move!"

"I know this van ain't bulletproof," I said. "I can tell by looking at it."

"So what?"

"Release him before we paint the inside with blood."

Instead of responding, they put the truck in drive and tried to use the van as a weapon.

"What a jackass," I said as I let my rounds go, spraying the driver and passenger.

The girls did their thing, too, because, by the time they opened the sliding door, everyone was gone, including Laytron. That smirk had long been wiped off his face. One of the bullets we sprayed hit him in the neck, shoulders, head, and wrist.

"Not how I expected it to go, but this will do," Sway said.

"Fuck!" Rel yelled as she paced back and forth. After mumbling something to herself, she ran over to the grass and threw up. It came out strong, like it came from a water hose.

"What now?" I asked, ignoring Rel's dramatic ass. She was all but rolling in the grass.

"I would say one of us drive the van, but it's too many bullet holes," Tweety said.

"Yeah, but it's night, and we can take some back roads."

"We can take Hampton all the way down to the intersection. I want to dump the bodies in front of the new club that's about to open. We need to show these Niggas who not to mess with.

As they contemplated what to do next, I opened the door to the van, stepping on glass. Snatching the mask off to see if I knew the faces, I jumped back. The driver had released himself and let out a sigh. I'd seen many dead bodies, so I didn't know why the very end of life still scared me. Everyone released themselves close to death. Some just did it sooner than others.

"Y'all know who these dudes is?" I asked.

"Nah, who?" Tweety asked.

"I don't know. That's why I asked y'all."

As I walked around to the back of the van, I saw a cop car coming at us at full speed. "Shit!" We had nowhere to go.

"Why we just sitting here like dumbasses? Damn," Tweety said.

"We're fucked." Rel dropped her gun and fell to her knees with her hands behind her head.

The cop car blocked us off, so now we had nowhere to run or hide. This was it.

The cop got out of the car. I couldn't see their face until she stood under the streetlights. Her hair was light brown and in finger waves. She had marked a beauty mole on her face like Lil' Kim did in her rap videos. Her light brown skin went with her light brown hair so well. The cop uniform fit every curve perfectly. She stood 5'6, taller than me. Her flashlight shined in our faces.

"Ladies. What have we here?"

"Officer, please, I can explain," Rel cried, running toward the van.

"Shut up, goofy. It's Asha," Sway said, giving Rel a confused look.

She looked at Rel in disbelief, and I knew why. If I didn't know any better, I would think Rel would've ratted us out if it wasn't Asha.

"What happened?" Asha walked around the truck. She then

used her radio to report no sign of a shooting on a different street, just to buy us time.

"Laytron robbed Rel," we said.

"Again?" Asha's eyes bucked, and she shook her at Rel. She looked at the bodies, trying to see if she knew who they were. She didn't.

"Yes, again," I said, still watching Sway as she watched Rel. I didn't even think Rel noticed that Sway hadn't taken her eyes off her.

"Take the back roads and ditch the van. It's a hostage situation north of Dallas, so it's safe. But you guys have to go now," Asha said before backing away to get into her patrol car.

"I'll take the van and dump it." Rel walked toward the driver's side.

"Hell no!" we all responded.

"We leave the rest of the bodies here. We take Laytron to club Obsessed, like I said."

We all looked at Sway like she was crazy. "We got the point across. No need for all that."

"But I want them homies of his not to be confused. They need to know we did it." She pointed at the other dudes. "Not these niggas."

Tired of arguing with her, I agreed, and we all dumped the irrelevant bodies from the van on the side of the street. We wouldn't be driving anywhere with those bodies. I drove the van, took it to a back road, and burned it. The girls picked me up, and we headed to the club.

Once at the club, I had a bad feeling about it. "They said the dude who owns this club is kinda a big deal. What if he don't appreciate how we used his new club for a public display?" I asked.

They dropped Laytron's body on the concrete. Instantly, Sway took pictures from a burner and sent them to the Messy Tea page in our city. The Messy page had all the latest tea, which gang was up on numbers, keeping track of the bodies dropping, and everything else. The last time Rel let the trap get robbed, I found out on the Messy Tea page first.

The night was crispy and warm, welcoming the summer. Judging by the body we'd just dropped at the club, this summer was about to be a long one.

As Sway boasted about the corpse she was responsible for, my phone rang. I stepped back to answer. "What's up, Asha? You okay?"

"Hey, you guys home?" She sounded like she was sneaking to talk.

"No. Why?"

"Why in the actual fuck did y'all throw the bodies on the curb?" She sounded stressed. Now I heard it—cameras flashing and reporters speaking.

The girls saw the troubled look on my face and neared me. Sway nodded. *What happened?* She mouthed.

I put the phone on speaker. "You there? Hello?" Asha asked.

"I'm here."

"I can only cover for you guys so much, but this was stupid. I told y'all to dump the bodies but not here." She exhaled a breath of frustration. "Listen, someone saw Mama Crystal's car. One of y'all burn the car but not before cleaning it. Then someone else make it to Mama Crystal before the cops do."

"How long we got?" Sway cut in.

"A little bit over an hour. It's a lot of bullet shells to pick up. I'm working the scene, so I'll toss out what I can. Fix this shit. Now."

The phone disconnected.

"I'll take care of the car," Tweety said. "After I'm done, I'll find a ride to my place."

"I'll take care of Mama Crystal," Rel said.

"Take care of her like how?" Sway asked.

Rel looked deeply confused. "I'm going to tell her not to speak to the cops."

We all shook our heads in disappointment. "I'll take care of

Mama Crystal," Sway said and then glanced over at Rel. "Rel is coming with me. I don't trust this hoe right now."

"Good," I said as I walked away.

Tweety drove away, and we all went our separate ways.

Once I got about a mile down, I stopped under the bridge with some homeless folks and called Terry to come scoop me. "Be there in ten," he said. Downtown wasn't far from me at all.

A lovely couple snuggled near the top of the bridge with the most cover. The man was asleep, but the woman stared at me. I smiled and walked over, then handed her a couple of hundreds.

"God bless you," she said, holding my hand long and tight.

At the bottom of the bridge, by the grass and trash bins, I waited for my ride. When I heard Lil Poppa's music blasting in the midnight air, I knew Terry was close. Once he pulled up in his Black Benz truck, I smiled and hopped inside.

He leaned over and kissed me, also blowing me a charge. "I can still smell the dead body on you," he said as he drove off. One hand was on the steering wheel, and the other passed me the blunt.

I took a puff and passed it back. "It's that loud?"

"Hell yeah." He coughed. "They just found a few bodies over by Redbird mall. That was y'all?"

"Long story."

"Make it short."

"We was only supposed to get Laytron."

"Dude that be sexing punks and taking they bread?" Everyone knew him for that.

"Yes. He robbed Rel."

"Again?" He shook his head, blowing out smoke. "Rel becoming a liability, ain't it?"

"Tell me why right when we was hopping out, a van pulled up and snagged him."

"So, y'all killed everyone in the van just to get Laytron?" He watched the road, but I could tell he was disappointed.

"Yes."

"Whose idea was that?"

I rolled my eyes. "You know whose idea it was."

"She becoming a liability too," he said, referring to Sway.

"At least I got her to chill out on the beef with y'all."

"Baby, that's light work. It ain't even no beef. Sway just annoying at this point. She dry droppin' bodies."

"In so many words, we all told her that. It was a vote."

"I know her narcissist ass hated that."

"That's still my friend. She's been through a lot. Stop."

He glanced over at me and wiped the smirk off his face. "I'm sorry, baby. Thank you for making her chill. I don't like drilling on women. That's lame to me."

We pulled up to the Omni and into the huge parking lot across the street. I started to get out, but Terry hated when I touched doors around him. In the streets, dude was a monster, but with me, he was soft as could be.

"You hungry?" he asked as we waited for the elevator to stop on the lobby level to pick us up.

"Yeah. Haven't really eaten anything. Fray came over early in the morning with that bull again."

Ding.

Terry let me walk inside first. He then pressed for us to go up to the very top floor. "He ain't touch you, did he?"

"No. He only be messing with Sway." I watched the uninterested look on his face and felt some type of way. "I know you don't like her, but every other week or so, I have to watch this man come over and do what he wants to my best friend, and it's nothing we can do about it. He knows it's nothing we can do about it."

Ding.

We walked out, and I followed him down the hall to the corner room, which was usually the biggest room on the floor. "Damn, that's crazy."

I walked into the spacious room and tossed my designer shoes near the kitchen. "Can you at least act like you care? He rapes her, you know?"

"Man, Sway a grown ass man. She'll be a'ight."

He extended his arm and led me to the back room. That's when I noticed rose petals. "What's going on, baby?"

"Just look." He pulled me inside the room to so many heart shaped balloons, rose petals, Hennessy, teddy bears, and other romantic things. One of the balloons read: WILL YOU BE MINE?

"I ain't gon' lie. I'm so in love with you, bruh. This thing so crazy." He got down on one knee.

"Oh my God!" I gave him my hand and tried to hold back tears. "Yes! Yes!"

He truly looked lost. Like he had no idea what was going on. "My blunt fell from my ear."

Sucking my teeth, I rolled my eyes and plopped down on the bed. "What's all this for?"

"For a minute now, we just been *kicking it,* and I ain't comfortable with that no more. I don't want to see you with nobody else. I'm tired of hearing about you with this dude and that dude. I know it be rumors, but I want you all to myself. I want you to officially be my girlfriend."

"What about the girls?"

"We can move slow on letting other people know, but as of right now, you mine." He yanked me off the bed and pulled me in for a juicy kiss.

"I'll be yours."

"I know you will. I wasn't asking." He kissed me again, but this time, he sucked on my bottom lip hard and rough like I liked it. "Now, bend over." He pulled his Polo shirt over his head and tossed it on the bed, leaving a whiff of his gratifying cologne as it landed next to me. "Show daddy you love him."

SWAY
MY NAME IS SWAY

Rel and I caught a ride back to Oakcliff by old-fashioned hitchhiking. Long ago, we learned the best way to avoid leaving trails when going places was to never, ever catch taxis or Ubers to or from doing dirty business. Hitchhiking was frowned upon because it was evil out there, and men waited for any and every chance to take advantage of *vulnerable* women. God bless any nigga who ever tried any of us because we didn't mind getting on demon time.

We were the girls the gremlins feared; they never knew what to expect.

Once we were dropped off on Mama Crystal's street, Rel gave me a look that I knew all too well. "You really starting to piss me off. Come on." I led the way down the street to Mama Crystal's house.

"Just try for once not killing. I'm starting to worry about you. It's a word for your mental disease."

I pulled my gun out as we walked to the side of the house. "Oh, yeah? What's that?" I asked, looking through the window.

Mama Crystal was in the kitchen with the phone between her ear and shoulder. From the looks of it, she was whipping up some good greens, neck bones, and macaroni and cheese. I sighed and slid my back down the bricks.

"It's called a sociopath." She snapped her fingers like she'd found a better word. "Psychopath, that's the name...." She went on and on about how I was the female Ted Bundy, except I wasn't sexually driven, and I wasn't a man.

"You're right."

She placed her hand in front of me like she was about to go off some more. "I don't want to hear it." Until she realized what I had just said, she kept going off. She then stopped and said, "You said what now?" as she kneeled next to me.

"I said you're right. She in there cooking, probably preparing to feed some kids. She don't deserve to die because you fucked up."

Rel stood and pointed at herself. "I fucked up?"

"If you hadn't been soft on Laytron and handled this shit when he did it the first time, we wouldn't be here."

With her arms crossed, she slid down next to me. "Facts." She couldn't even deny it.

"What we do now?"

"We go inside and explain to her what happened. We tell her to report her car stolen and we will replace it by the end of the week. Then we tell her that her secrecy will be highly appreciated."

"You know I love me some Mama Crystal," I admitted.

She stood and pulled me up too. "I know."

We then dusted ourselves off. Before walking to the front door, I placed my gun back into my purse. I had my small gun. Tweety already knew to destroy the big ones; they were evidence now.

Mama Crystal finally opened the door. The first thing she did was look over our shoulders. When she didn't see her car, she mugged us and said into the phone, "Let me call you back."

I'm doing a good deed.
I'm doing a good deed.

I'm doing a good deed.

Mama Crystal's house was like the candy house. It was so cozy and full of any snack you could think up. She knew how to finesse the government, so she had some stacks coming in just off food stamps. For her to be a junkie, she never went without a house or a car. Those were mandatory.

"So, that *was* y'all," she said with her arms folded.

We both walked into the living room and sat on the comfortable sofa. "What?" I asked.

She jerked her head sideways. "Don't insult my intelligence, Sway. The police already came by, asking me about my car and why it was seen at a murder."

I let my head fall into my hands, almost smothering my nose. "What you tell them?" I asked, sounding muffled.

She looked at me like I knew better than to ask that. "What you mean *what I tell them*? I told them my car was in the driveway the last time I saw it. I reported it stolen."

I exhaled a breath of pure relief. With sad eyes, I glanced up at her. I couldn't believe I had almost killed my favorite person in the world. With thankful eyes, I smiled at Rel. She smiled back. I was sure she knew what I was thinking.

"Please don't fuss, Mama Crystal. I'm getting you a better car at the end of the week."

"Oh, I know. Tuh. I'm hearing my car had all types of bullet holes in it."

We all shared a laugh. "No, that was the van. Your car was fine. Just had to get rid of it."

"I ain't asking no questions, child." She tossed her hands up and quickly moved to the kitchen. "Y'all want a hot plate?"

When I finally made it home, Spin's jeep was nowhere to be found. Before going inside, I took Rel home, then came back and sat in the car. Pulling out my phone, I smiled at my screensaver, which was a screenshot of the last message from Houston. The last message he sent said: ***I got a headache, baby. Can u rub my head when I get home?***

With slow music still playing, I scrolled through pictures. He was so handsome. His perfect brown skin, dimples, high-top fade, and beautiful smile were all I thought about. Houston knew how to handle me. He knew me way before I became Sway. Houston knew me when I simply went by my government name, Katie Vermont. When I was still a pissy teenager who didn't know how to tell my teacher my period had started, he would steal my sanitary napkins from the store. He stole them in bulk because he hated being seen with them. So he minimized the number of visits he would have to make.

A knock at my window startled me nearly to death. My eyes were on the man standing at my window, but I couldn't focus because my mind was focused on my hand reaching for my gun.

"You won't need that," the man said in a calm voice. He stepped to the side to show me a black SUV parked on the side of me. "Mr. Delyle would like to speak with you."

I rolled the window all the way down. "Who's Mr. Delyle?"

"Would you mind?" He gestured toward the door handle. I opened it, being sure to let him see the gun in my hand. He visibly tried to keep from laughing. "Come." He opened the back door to the SUV.

"Am I supposed to get in?"

"You will get in."

"Tuh."

"Don't make this hard. Please." He was so polite. Something about his manners sent a chill down my spine, and that wasn't always easy. I didn't want to get in the back seat, but something told me I didn't have a choice.

I grabbed my phone, keeping my gun in hand, and got out of the car. He bowed toward the door as I got in, and he closed it behind me. My attention was too focused on the man outside to notice that I was now in the presence of someone. I jerked around. He leaned over, pressing the button to let the window down. He then grabbed my gun with ease and placed it in the hands of the man outside the door.

"She won't be needing this." His scent was soft and manly.

When he leaned back over, I got a good look at him. He was dressed in a tailored suit as if he'd just left a very important meeting with very important people. His hair was cut low, even all around, and wavy. Judging by the crispness of his edge up, he'd recently gotten a cut.

"Why am I here?" I asked. Of course, I had an attitude. I'd basically been forced into the car.

"You seemed to have left something at the entrance of my club. I need it gone by the morning."

Rolling my eyes, I said, "I don't know what you're talking about."

Though I tried to avoid eye contact with him, his eyes never left me. I didn't know exactly who he was, but I had an idea. "Don't insult my intelligence. If I'm here and you're here, then it's for a reason."

"Tuh."

"I want it gone by sunrise."

"Yeah, we'll see." I placed my hand on the door, but he snatched me by the arm. I tried to swing at him, but so many lasers appeared out of nowhere. All were on different parts of my body, coming from outside the car. I had no idea where the men who held the guns were.

He grabbed my fist and placed it in my lap. "I seriously wouldn't do that if I were you. And please do not ever try it again. I won't ask twice. I want it gone by morning."

"You a cop?"

"I'm the sole owner of Club Obsessed."

"How'd you find me?"

"Trust me, it wasn't hard. You sent a picture of the body to a Facebook page, for Christ's sake. Your actions are disgusting." He looked repulsed, as if my style was beneath him. "You're not too smart."

"Fuck off." I turned to get out, but he placed his hand on my shoulder.

"Get it done."

I didn't say anything. Just nodded and slammed the door once I was out. After my gun was returned, the SUV left. Minutes later, many other cars followed from all over the street.

He seemed to be a big deal but fuck that. *My name is Sway. No man gon' punk me.*

I went into the house and got myself ready for bed. I would sleep like a baby. No man in a tailored suit who used words like *disgusting* to describe me would get the satisfaction of seeing me sweat.

That body would be there when the sun came up until he or the police moved it.

Asha
All Is Fair In War

My colleagues were going crazy over the radios. Being that I worked the night shift, I was on duty when a tip came from a Facebook group about a body lying in front of a club that hadn't even opened yet. The entire way there, I blew up every one of the Spindarellas' phones, but no one answered. The one I called back-to-back was Sway. This had her fucking name written all over it.

Though I was one of the founding members, I chose to be a cop. I chose to be a cop for many reasons. The main reason was that I was the laidback type growing up and still was, so people really didn't know I was part of a gang. I used the streets' ignorance as a gain and joined the Dallas Police Department. It gave us leverage, but there was only so much I could do without bringing an eye on myself. Thank God my girls knew that. For example, I was working alongside a partner one day, and he ended up pulling over Spin and Sway. I was forced to give them a ticket and rough them up a bit, but we all laughed about it later. They understood sacrifices had to be made for this to work.

It was six in the morning, so I knew someone was up, yet no one was answering the phone. This was beyond annoying.

When I exited the highway, I glanced at the entrance and thought I was tripping when I didn't see anything. I then drove closer, but still nothing. So, I parked and used my flashlight. Though daylight was breaking, it was still a bit dark.

I saw nothing, not even behind the bushes. No clothing. No blood. No body. But what I did smell was bleach and something else I couldn't explain.

The large glass door to the luxury club came open, and out walked a cop who worked the same shift as me. "Hey, Dennis, I didn't know you called in to the scene," I said as I put my flashlight into its holding place on my thick belt.

Dennis was what people would call a *cool cop*. Didn't write many tickets, had lots of respect in the streets, and actually wanted to help the youth as opposed to just locking them up. He was a football player in high school and made it all the way to the NFL, just to tear his ACL the first year. Standing at 5'11 sharp, he had brown skin the color of Twix. He wore his hair in a mini fro of small dreads and always kept an edge up. His teeth were perfect, and he still had the body of a football player. Mainly because he hit the gym every single day.

"That's because I didn't. I was in the area, so I decided to stop and see what the picture was about."

"And?"

He extended both hands, looking at the ground where the body was supposed to be. "Not here. It was some kind of sick prank. Maybe they photoshopped the body. Who knows?"

"So, everything is good?" I asked as I saw another man walking out.

He was tall, chocolate, and handsome. Looked to be about forty exactly. He was what the girls my age would call a *zaddy*. His salt and pepper beard was trimmed to perfection.

Dennis turned around, then clapped hands and bumped shoulders with the man. "Yeah, it's all good. This here is the owner. He was a longtime friend of my late father."

The man grabbed my hand with both hands and smiled. "I'm Delyle. It's nice to meet you."

"I'm Asha, but in uniform, I'm Officer Wynn. I hear someone played a bad joke on you."

He laughed, scratching his beard. I almost missed it, but he clenched his jaw. He was laughing to keep from showing how upset he was. "It's fine. I've been on the butt end of better jokes."

"Ha, some joke," I said.

"Right, some joke," he responded.

Dennis got called on the radio, so he walked away to answer it. Yes, I was a cop, but I was a street bitch who could read between the lines. "Do you know who I am?" I asked, only loud enough for Delyle to hear.

Without any emotions, he said, "Yes."

I looked to make sure Dennis was still far enough away. "You cleaned it up?"

"I had my men do it. I gave your friend until daybreak to get him from my club."

"She didn't do it?"

"No. She laughed in my face." He had a heavy Jamaican accent.

I knew a dangerous man when I encountered one, and this one made the hairs stand up on the back of my neck. The fact that he was older meant he was smart enough to stand the test of time. There was no sign of that body. He'd done this before, and he'd been doing it for a while.

"I want to apologize for her. Is there anything I can do to fix this?"

"You can bring her to me."

I took a few steps back and swallowed the lump in my throat. "Excuse me?"

"You can bring her to me," he said in a monotone. He didn't even blink when he said it the first time or the second.

"I—I can't do that."

"Then there's nothing you can do for me." He turned to walk away, but I stopped him.

"Wait." He turned to face me with both hands now in his pants pockets. "Are you going to hurt her?"

"No. She's just going to be taught a very valuable lesson." This time, he walked back inside.

I could live with him teaching her a lesson. Sway was a tough one. His not killing her was great because deep down inside, I knew we wouldn't even survive the beginning of a war with him. His aura did all the speaking, and I still was scared, which was hard to do. Me, Spin, Sway, and Tweety had all been through so much, so putting fear in us would take work, and he did it with ease. The fact that he even got close enough to Sway to demand she do something said a lot.

As I strolled to my patrol car, Dennis walked over. "About to clock out?" he asked, holding the door open for me.

"Yeah, been a long night."

"You can say that again." He closed the door and tapped the hood. "Get some rest."

"You, too."

After driving away, I called Sway over and over but still got no answer.

Did he already get her? I asked myself, then quickly blew it off. He wouldn't have asked me to bring her if he had.

I looked down at the clock and saw that I had no more time left. Since I wasn't working a scene, I had to go and clock out. The station was downtown, not far from where I was.

After clicking out, I went to the parking garage across the street where my car was and called Sway again. Still got no answer.

Fuck it. I would just have to go over there.

On the way to the loft, Spin finally called me back. "Where the fuck is Sway?" I answered.

Yawning, she said, "Should be home."

"You ain't there?"

"Nah, I'm with Terry."

That didn't surprise me since I was the only one of the Spindarellas who knew of them two messing around.
"Whose idea was the whole club thing?"
"You know whose idea it was."
"I just had to be sure." I hung up.

I loved my girls dearly, especially the ones I had known since childhood—like Sway—but this had to either slow down or stop. My job would be on the line soon if I didn't put a handle on this. Or worse, they would bring all of us under investigation.

To be real, the Spindarellas weren't a problem for me in the beginning. Slowly, it became a problem. For one, Sway seemed to have lost her mind. I wanted to blame it on her losing Houston, but no. She was popping off way before then. The whole situation with Houston and her baby just made things way worse. She had put us in so much unnecessary beef that I had lost count. Sway was always talking about how someone needed to be disciplined when in actuality, the main one who needed to be reprimanded was *her*.

Spin got her name because she was in the streets before any of us. She had to be. But Sway was the one who did most of the spinning. It was starting to draw attention, and she wanted it to draw attention. That's the part that upset me.

The beef with the SAD boys was all Sway. She started it. If it wasn't for the soft spot Terry held for Spin, they would've had most of us wiped out by now. Nobody, and I do mean *nobody*, just woke up one day and decided to beef with Terry and 'em. It was plain suicide. Sway acted like she was built Ford tough, but to be real, I think she did all that extra shit because she knew the guys in the game would take it easy on us because we were good-looking. That's the only thing I could come up with. Nobody could be *this* out of their mind.

When I got to the loft, I beat on the door as loud as I could without causing a disturbance. When she didn't answer, I used my key.

As I ran to her room, my heart pounded. I had no idea what I would find, but all I found was her asleep. Sighing, I snatched the covers off and stood over her, so she could see who it was. Her head jerked toward the door and the window until her eyes finally landed on me. "Are you crazy?" she asked in a groggy voice.

"I was about to ask you the same thing. Get up!" I yelled.

She rolled her eyes and laid back down, so I snatched her by her arm and yanked her out of bed. She tried to swing, but I was too fast. I caught her with a two-piece, sending her right back down to the bed.

Growing up, Sway and I would always get into fist fights, and I would always win. On the real, it was only two other members who could even touch me, and one was a guy for real. From the shoulders, I was guaranteed to knock someone out. That's why being a cop came natural to me. I could shoot it out, of course, but nobody was about to overpower me.

I didn't even know why Sway even tried it.

"Are you crazy? It's too fucking early," she said, sitting at the edge of the bed and catching her breath.

"Why would you leave a body in front of a club and then send it to a Facebook page?" I was now in her face. "If you have a death or jail wish, then cool, but bitch, you ain't taking all of us down."

She blew me off and walked to the kitchen. I followed her. "Your job is to make sure we don't end up in jail."

"That's what I do off the strength, but it's *not* my job! My job is to protect and serve the innocent. Last night, someone broke into an elderly woman's house, raped her, and robbed her. We found him within an hour. That's my job!"

She clapped her hands and took a sip of orange juice. "Good for you."

I snatched the orange juice from her. "Do you have any concern for that man?"

"Who?" She looked concerned. "The asshole who came by, attempting to threaten me?" she arrogantly asked.

"The owner of the club. I was called in to the scene this morning, but he'd already cleaned it up for you. You dragged him into your shit, Katie." Whenever I called her by her government, she knew nothing was a game.

"Fuck him. How did he even know who I was?"

Shrugging, I said, "I don't know. Same way he knew how to find you last night."

"I don't know. He just popped up. Next thing I knew, beams were on me, and he was demanding I clean the body."

"And you thought you'd laugh in his face and not do it?"

"Yes."

"But, why not? At least he kept it in the streets and didn't turn you in. The very least you could've done was cleaned your mess. It was careless."

"You're starting to piss me off. All you do is bitch and whine. Like, girl, shut the fuck up." She snatched the orange juice back.

I was done trying to talk sense into her. It was all on her at this point. Snatching my keys off the counter, I rolled my eyes and stomped away. She made sure to slam the door behind me.

Once in the car, I called Spin. "Hey, you find her?"

"Yeah," I said, "but that's not why I called. If Sway goes missing for a day or two, don't go looking for her. She'll turn back up. Might turn back up with a few bruises, but she will be okay."

"What? Why?"

"That guy who owns the club. His name is Delyle. He asked her to clean up the body before daybreak, and she laughed in his face. He had it cleaned himself, but he's not too happy about it."

"What if he kills her?"

"Trust me, he's not going to kill her. I can just tell. But if we get in the way of him teaching her a lesson, I think this will be the one beef that we don't make it back from."

"Is he plugged in?"

"Spin, I think he *is* the man that niggas get plugged in with. Something tells me we shouldn't get in his way."

"Give me your word that you don't think he will kill her."

"You have my word. Just stand down and act like you ain't know."

She let out a nervous breath. "Okay, bet."

I felt bad about this, but it had to be done. At the end of the day, Sway was due to run into her match sooner or later. Good thing was, at least he decided to handle it instead of calling the cops. Bad thing was... he decided to handle it.

But all is fair in war.

Sway
Afraid Of The Dark

There was darkness all around me. I couldn't see anything at all with whatever was thrown over my head.

A little bit after Asha left, I showered and got dressed, preparing to make my rounds in the streets and check on the trap houses, but someone snatched me up and tossed me into a van with something thrown over my head. From what I could gather with my senses, only two men were in the van with me—the man driving and the man holding me down, placing zip ties on my hands and feet. They spoke amongst each other in another language.

"Do you know what the fuck I do? Do you know who I am?" I asked as I tried so desperately to free myself. "Let me go!"

The man in the back of the van with me bellowed with laughter. "You're so cute."

"Cute? I'll show you cute." I kicked, and when I felt his hand, I bit it.

"Oh, no, she bit me." Both men burst into laughter together.

"What's going on?"

"Should've just cleaned the body up like he asked. Boss is a good man."

Then it dawned on me. "Delyle?" Instantly, everything

around me got more and more intense. All I could see in the darkness was his face when he told me I had until daybreak to clean up the body.

"Shhhhh. You'll see him soon enough."

"I'm going to kill you all! All of you....." I went on and on with threats that I fully planned to follow through on.

In the background, I couldn't help but hear the sound of a zipper, like someone had opened a bag. Then I heard a case open and close.

"Hold still," he said. Then he pricked my arm with a sharp needle, it seemed.

"No," I whimpered as I felt myself losing control and falling out.

A splash of water woke me from a slumber that I had no idea I'd even fallen into. One minute, I was in the back of a van, and the next, I was in an extremely neat and clean dungeon. I had on nothing but my bra and panties with both hands chained above me. My legs were held in place by foot shackles.

The dungeon was clearly in the basement of something and had black marble floors with all black walls. There was an all-black love seat in front of me. "Aaaaaaahhhhhh! Help! Help me!"

I heard the echo of a laugh behind me. "I didn't take you as the type to scream for help."

I couldn't turn around, but he slowly walked in front of me. It was Delyle. Instead of his fancy suit, he wore black joggers with no shirt, revealing his perfect body.

"Fuck you."

He sat down on the love seat and used a remote control. He pressed a button, and suddenly my arms started to stretch. "No." I frantically looked up to see what was happening. "Please, it hurts. No. No!"

He stopped and pressed another button, making me comfortable again. I exhaled in relief. "You will watch your language in my home." I started to spit on him, but I was afraid of what he would do. I didn't like the thought of being stretched to death. It seemed like a sadistic way to die.

"Okay."

He leaned forward on his elbows like he was about to ask me some very important questions. "We seem to have a bit of confusion going on."

"Can you let me down?" I asked. I was tired of not being able to rest properly. The shackles around my feet and ankles were killing me.

"Why didn't you get the body like I asked? I thought I showed you a great deal of courtesy and respect. You get in my car with a gun, laugh in my face, and leave the body in front of my business. Do you understand why you're here? Or should I continue?" I didn't answer, so he pressed the button and stretched me more this time.

"Stop! Please!"

"Answer me."

"No, I understand. I know why I'm here, and I'm sorry. I'm so sorry." I was now sweating bullets, it seemed. Sweat came from all over my body.

"I had to postpone the opening of my club because what? Because you wanted to prove a point to some petty thief and his friends?" He stood and was now in my face. "You think I'm one of them?" His chilling tone and hot breath against the side of my neck made my body quiver.

"Who are you?"

He wasn't a regular club owner. No, this man had pull. I'd never heard of him, but he freely roamed the crime-infested streets of Dallas, Texas, picking citizens off the street like candy and tossing them into dungeons. He'd clearly done this before, possibly over a dozen times. He did it with such balance and ease.

"I know who *you* are. I ask the questions. Not you." He sat back in the love seat and let his eyes roam my body.

"This what this is about? Just fuck me and get it over with."

"If I wanted to fuck you, I would've fucked you the two days you've been knocked out."

"Excuse me?" I couldn't have heard him right. "What did you just say?"

"You've been here two days. My men miscalculated the amount of drugs put into the syringe. For that, I deeply apologize."

I was still stuck on the two days. I wanted to flash out so bad, but it would be pointless. I didn't want to die down there. "What do you want from me?" Men always wanted something from women. It was never anything that didn't come with a catch.

"How does it make you feel when you kill someone?"

"I need water."

He stepped back like that was the wrong answer. Suddenly, the lights went off, and it was pitch black. "You're not ready." I heard his bare feet walking up the stairs.

"Wait, please don't leave me like this. Please, no. I'll do anything. I will answer your questions."

"I'll try again tomorrow."

"Tomorrow!"

The only light I saw was the glimpse he gave me when he opened the door to the basement and closed it.

SPIN
Wrong Idea

"It's been two days, Asha. Something has to be wrong." I was pacing all over Terry's apartment. Though Terry lived in Ft Worth, where most of our opps lived, we were good. Nobody messed around with anything that belonged to him, whether it was a thing, animal, or person.

His huge, muscular pit bull lazily watched from the couch as I panicked.

"Come on, Diamond. Come eat." Terry set a full bowl of raw meat by the back door.

"We should just go up there," Asha said.

"No, we can't do that. What if he kills us?"

Terry shook his head and continued cooking the burger patties he was making for us. "You sure it's the dude from the club who got her?" I asked for the thousandth time.

"I'm sure. Look, they haven't found the body, so she's still alive."

"And what if she's not?" I asked. "Do we go after him?"

"Let's not skip to any conclusion." I could tell she was over it because she stood and grabbed her bag. "I'll skip out on the burgers."

"Where you going?" I asked.

"Home. It's the only off day I have this week, so I want to enjoy it." She walked toward the door like she'd had it with everything for the day. Her head was shaking left to right. She finally stopped and turned toward me. "I love my sister, too, you know?"

Confused, I said, "I know."

"But I'm not about to let her get any of us killed. When she's back home, I advise you to never let her know we knew about this. She will hate us forever."

"I won't."

She half smiled and walked away.

"What was that all about?" I asked myself aloud.

"Seems to me Asha is about sick and tired of Sway." Terry slid a water bottle next to my plate of food.

"We're all sick of Sway, but that's not a reason to want her dead. You know?"

"She's not dead."

"You sound so sure."

"I am sure."

SWAY
HELL ON EARTH

The sudden brightness flashed, causing me to squint my eyes in pain. I hadn't noticed I was sleeping until the pain in my neck reminded me I had been hanging my head down for hours. The pain of it all caused me to scream. "Ahhhhh!"

He came over to me, causing me to flinch. "Relax." He gently placed his hand under my chin and lifted my head. "Drink." I turned my head. "Either drink or I go back upstairs and leave you down here for another three days."

Reluctantly, I drank the water and snatched my head away from him. Suddenly, my hands were no longer above my head, and my legs weren't spread apart. My body fell to the hard flood on all fours. "Fuck!" I heard my knee pop.

Any other time I would've looked for anything around me to fight him with, but I had no energy. In a few short seconds, my body turned to Jell-O, and I fell completely on my stomach.

"Just let me go."

"When I'm ready."

"What do you want? Just fuck me and get it over with," I said just above a whisper.

"I wouldn't touch you, especially not in this state. You smell like a fish market."

"I haven't showered."

"I'm aware." He walked over, pulled me up to a foldable chair, and slung me into it like a rag doll. He then sat on his love seat and pulled my chair closer to him.

"What do you want?"

"I want you to understand that I'm not one of these local thugs shooting over territory and colors. I'm a grown ass man, and you *will* respect me. Even when I let you go. If you come back around looking for trouble, I will give you trouble."

I wanted to tell him to fuck off, but I was afraid of being hung in the middle of the room again. "Fine."

"I can break you down. I can break you down to nothing. I don't have to kill you." He tossed me a big towel and a small one. "The shower is in the corner."

Slowly, I looked back and saw a large shower head in the corner of the basement with drains under it. "Where's the shower curtain?"

"Don't have one."

I nodded and walked over to the shower, taking my clothes off as I walked. Since I didn't have any physical weapons, I would use my sexy body. It never failed me.

The water ran over my hair and body as I watched him from the corner of my eye. He didn't seem impressed. In fact, he glanced down at his watch quite a bit, as if he was pressed for time. For me to be reduced to showering in an open basement, it was nice down there. Even the shower was nice. The soap smelled of lavender and jasmine. I almost forgot I had a one man audience.

"I don't mean to interrupt your *me time*, but can you speed this up? I want to get you back home before dark."

"Home?" I asked.

There had to be a catch. He didn't want sex? He had me in his basement alone, and he could've done anything to me, but he was about to take me home?

"Yes, home."

"So, that's it? You kept me down here for days, just to put a crook in my neck?"

"To show you how easy you are to touch. You gave me the impression that you thought nobody could touch you. I guess this was a reality check." The water hit my back as I watched him with anger. I was angry at him and myself. Angry at him for keeping me down there for no reason. Angry at myself for being angry at all. I should've been happy. He watched my back like he could see my thoughts with captions. He read right through me. "Ohhhh, it bothers you that someone doesn't want you. Doesn't it?"

"No. I just—I thought—I don't know what I thought." I was going home with nothing but a headache and a stiff neck. I should've been very grateful, so why was I furious? "You called me disgusting the other day."

"I didn't call you disgusting. I used that word to describe an action of yours that I found unpleasant."

"Same thing."

He walked over to me and stood there. His body was stiff as a statue. The muscles on him looked hard as a rock with his thick veins poking out. I couldn't breathe for a moment. I could feel his breath on my body.

"I can do whatever I want to you right now, but what fun is that?" He leaned down toward me, and my body stiffened.

I closed my eyes, preparing for a kiss, but instead, I heard the knob turning. When I opened my eyes, he was walking back toward the love seat. He'd only come over to turn the water off, further rushing me to finish, so he could get me home.

After I dried off, he tossed me some small sweatpants with a muscle tee. They still had tags on them, so he'd just bought them just for me. "I hope you don't mind. I tossed your other clothes out. They were soiled."

"It's fine," I said as I sat back down in the foldable chair. "What did you do with the body?"

"It's burned to ashes. They'll never find him. Why would a woman like you want to kill that dude? From what I've heard, he isn't on your level. He seemed to be a petty thief."

I sighed. "He was on the downlow and dating a friend of mine. Well, he robbed her a couple of times, and I felt like he would keep doing it."

"So, you killed him?"

He looked at me like he further disapproved of my decision-making. I sat upright, preparing to defend my actions. "Well, yeah. I had to, or he would've kept doing what he was doing. We're already women in a man's territory. You know? Now they will know not to fuck with us."

He slowly lifted his head up and down, letting me know I had made a valid point. But, for some reason, I felt it wasn't valid enough. "They're still going to rob you and your friends. Just now, they won't leave anyone alive when they do."

I slammed my back against the seat. "Okay, so what was I supposed to do?"

"There are things on earth worse than death."

"Like what?"

"Hell."

I rolled my eyes. "Mothafucka would have to die to get to hell."

He extended his hand to mine to help me up. "With a mindset like you have, you won't make it past twenty-five."

"What's that supposed to mean?" I was now following him up the stairs, anxious for his answer. "You seem to have so much to say about my methods."

"Your neck isn't hurting anymore. Is it?"

Stunned, I rubbed my neck. "Actually, no. How did you know?"

"The soap you used to shower has CBD in it and other things that relax the body."

"Why is that in the basement?"

He winked at me and opened the basement door, leading me through the marvelous, humongous kitchen. A cook passed me something in foil as I walked by her. As if she knew I was in the basement and knew he would be releasing me. I opened the foil and saw a well filled breakfast sandwich.

"Wow, thanks," I said to him as we walked through the foyer.

"No problem." He opened the front door. "My driver will take you home or wherever you want to go."

I stood there in disbelief. "Is he going to kill me?"

He grabbed the bridge of his nose. "I'm a man of my word. I know that means nothing these days, but I said I wouldn't hurt you, and I meant it."

"What if I was to come back and kill you?"

"You wouldn't."

"But how do you know?"

"Trust me. I know these things." He nodded toward the SUV. "He's waiting."

Frozen, I thought about all that could go wrong. "Why do I feel like I'll never be seen again once I get into the SUV?" He leaned against the wall and smiled at me. It was a mischievous grin, but something had intrigued him. "What?" I wanted to know what was so interesting to him.

"You're terrified."

"And you're crazy. A different type of crazy."

"So, we agree on something."

"I don't want to go. I want *you* to take me."

"Why? You think if I take you, then I won't get you killed? Get in the truck." He wasn't asking. He was telling me.

I took a deep breath and walked to the truck, looking back at him. Quickly, I slid into the back of the truck just in case someone tried to knock me over the head.

The driver and Delyle looked at each other and laughed.

As the SUV drove away, I found myself wanting to know more about this Delyle. Who was he? How did he know so much? How many bodies had he made disappear? Would I be the next body to never be seen again?

I didn't know, but I was sure about to find out. If I made it through this day, Delyle would see me again.

I sat back in the seat and tried to register what had just happened. Usually, my seduction would've worked, but it didn't need to work. I wanted to be in his mind. He wasn't afraid of me —the girl who dropped a dead body in front of his establishment. He didn't bat a lash.

The driver had been staring at me through the middle rear view. "Can I help you?" I asked.

"You're confused. Aren't you?"

"Very."

"Just be happy you and your friends get to live life as you know it. Take this as a lesson to show respect in order to get respect."

"My friends?"

"Yes. Be happy he didn't change all of you."

"What does that even mean?"

The driver laughed and fixed the rear view, now focusing on the road. "He was annoyed. Not angry. Don't make him angry and pray you never find out."

CRYSTAL
THE CARE TAKER

From the window of my house, I watched Terry as he sat in his car, contemplating whether he wanted to deal with the burst of emotions today. This was regular for him. Every other day, he came by to check on his mother, who lived next door.

His mother, Icis, was the sweetest woman alive but her addiction to heroin was nasty. Anyone who tried to help her, she resented. So, instead of forcing her into rehabs, which she always ran away from, he decided to keep her safe while she indulged.

I had just gotten home from working my overnight shift, so my nursing uniform was still on. My tennis shoes were still laced, so I made my way outside. He saw me walking to the car and unlocked the passenger side door.

He was laid way back in the seat and looking over at me with exhaustion written all over his face. "Good morning," I said as I leaned over to kiss him, but he slightly turned his head. "I gotta get used to that. I'm sorry."

Terry and I had been together for almost six years, and one day, he woke up and decided he didn't love me anymore. The confusion still killed me on the inside because I didn't know what I had done. I still didn't know. My brother, who was a cop in

Dallas, told me I needed to let my love for Terry go. He said it was things that he didn't want me dragged into.

There were rumors about some girl he was messing with from Dallas. I heard she was a Spindarella, but with he say and she say, there was never a way to really know.

"She okay?" he asked, referring to his mother.

"Yes. I went in last night before work and changed out all her needles. I also stocked the fridge with groceries and water. I remember you saying you wanted her to drink more water. With the extra money you gave me, I also bought a tracker and stitched it to the inside of her purse just in case she tries to pull a disappearing act again."

He sighed and faced directly ahead. "You made sure she got pure drugs and nothing with fentanyl?"

I nodded. "Yes. I also watered it down a little bit with what you asked and put more morphine than heroin. She won't be able to tell the difference." Being that I was a nurse, I had access to morphine and other things. "I'm getting to the point where it's mostly morphine, so she will be off heroin sooner or later. This was a great way to go about it." He looked so down every time he came to see her. It's like Icis drained the life out of him.

"You need anything?" he asked.

He always asked this. Though we were over, he always asked this whenever he stopped by. He took good care of me, and I took good care of him. That's all we did for each other.

"I'm okay. Just need to get my air conditioner fixed. It's blowing out warm air instead of cold."

He pulled out a roll of money and put it in my lap. I put it back in his lap. "I'll pay for it."

He placed it back in my lap. "Don't do this today. Take the money. If you don't use it for the air, use it to take yourself somewhere nice or take Icis somewhere nice. It's yours, do what you please."

I slid it into my bra. "You don't have to keep giving me money."

"I know. Just like you don't have to look out for Icis for me, but you do anyway. Thank you."

"I do it because I love you, and I love her." He remained silent. He never indulged when I leaned toward romance with him. "How are you doing? How's Diamond?"

"She's good. I think I need to start back feeding her dog food. She bit my neighbor the other day, and I had to pay him not to rat me out."

"Once they taste blood, it's over."

"I might have to put her down. She keeps trying to attack people."

"Just bring her here for a week. I'll bring her back to reality. You have her around men all day who play rough with her and laugh when she attacks. She needs to be cuddled and softly talked to, not treated as a fight dog."

He grinned. "You too good for this earth, Crystal."

"Then why did you leave me?" I couldn't help it. I had been walking on eggshells around him for months, denying myself the proper closure, just to make him more comfortable.

"We'll talk about it later."

"Terry, please. I haven't had a good night's sleep in months, and I just want to know what I did that was so wrong?"

"We're just not compatible in a relationship anymore. We're better off as friends, and you know that."

"One day, we're making love and watching scary movies in the living room, and the next day I come home, and all of your stuff is gone." Exhaling slowly, I tried to keep from crying. Crying never worked with him. He hated it.

"You deserve better than me. You deserve a man who's ready to give you a family, marriage, and a huge house with a white picket fence. That just ain't me."

"I can wait for you."

"That's the problem. You're always trying to put your happiness aside for me. I want you to go and find that man. I want you to be happy."

"But, Terry, baby, you make me happy. I'm not ready for all that family stuff either."

"Yes, you are, and you know it. I love you enough to let you go. This is the purest form of love I've ever had for anyone." He gently grabbed my chin. "I don't want anything standing in the middle of your joy, not even me."

"Is it true?"

"Is what true?"

"The girl from Dallas?"

"What good would it be for me to answer that? It's not changing anything between you and me. I'm still here for you. I still love you. It won't help."

"So, it is true." He lazily moved his hand to the keys that were still in the ignition and started the car. "Wait, you're not going to see Icis? She's been asking about you."

"I'll come by tonight." He knew I wouldn't be there tonight.

"Terry, please. Just tell me what I need to do, and I'll do it. I'll do anything."

"Right now?"

"Yes." I nodded with a frown.

He leaned over and opened the passenger door. The pain traveled from my throat all the way to the pit of my stomach and then to my feet. This was why I sometimes avoided these types of conversations, too, because they always ended like this.

"I'm sorry, Crystal. I really am."

Using the knuckle of my index finger to wipe a tear before it fell, I said, "It's fine. I shouldn't have pushed the issue." I got out and closed the door behind me.

He waited until I got inside before he drove away. Once I was sure he'd left, I broke down against the door and let out months' worth of tears.

I couldn't win for losing with that man.

ASHA
No Need to say Thank You

Spin was the first to call me when it happened. Sway had reappeared at home, and everything seemed to be fine. Of course, Spin avoided direct contact with her for obvious reasons.

"I haven't been in her room. She's cleaning up with loud music playing. I tried to offer her breakfast, but she was already eating a breakfast sandwich."

That wasn't like Sway, and everyone knew. To know Sway, then you had to know how unusual that was of her.

It had been three days since Sway had been home, and nothing had changed. She still was quiet. Still was easy going. Even when she checked on the trap in South Dallas, only to find out that the junkie we paid to clean it had actually stolen a few hundreds of dollars worth of work, Sway didn't go off the deep end. She simply said she was inventing new ways of dealing with trouble. Later that day, the junkie went missing, and we found out Sway put her in a rehab facility. We asked why, we all asked why, multiple times and had yet to get an answer.

"The streets think you got the junkie killed," I told her.

"Good. It's part of the plan. So, when she reappears, they will know that I showed her mercy. They will also know that mercy is a silent warning not to fuck me twice. Because if she fucks me after I tried to help, I will be under the impression that rehab didn't work because that's who she is inside. Then I won't blame it on the drugs." She said that earlier this morning, and I still couldn't wrap my head around what the fuck was going on with her.

It was my off day, and we all decided to go out tonight and shut the city down. We shut all the traps down in celebration of Sway being back home. The ones closest to her, we knew where she'd been. We knew before she told us. We had to act like we didn't. The rest of the clique and everyone else didn't know. They thought she was out of town.

Club Obsessed was due to open tonight. He'd prolonged it to get the buzz back going, which didn't surprise me. What surprised me was Sway telling us Club Obsessed would be the move for tonight.

"But you said Delyle took you. Are you sure you want to go?" we asked her.

"He didn't kill me."

"It doesn't matter," Spin said. "He took you."

"Listen, this night is about me, and that's where I want to be. Okay?"

We all agreed with much resistance. I think everyone else was afraid of what I was afraid of—we didn't want him to mention to Sway that we all knew he would take her and didn't try to stop it.

Needless to say, we stood outside our cars, fixing our club outfits, hair, and makeup. The pink and blue neon lights mixed with the music and other people had us feeling good. We all were nervous but still felt good.

Sway waited patiently for a few more members to pull up while the rest of us chattered amongst each other. I watched from the corner of my eye as Sway looked at the humongous club like she longed to be inside it. It wasn't a hateful look, which sent me in many confusing directions mentally. I wanted to know what happened to her in that dungeon and if she was telling us everything. Her nude-colored dress, red heels, and freshly retwisted locs let me know she indeed wanted to look perfect tonight.

While everyone was talking, I eased behind her and checked her body for weapons like a cop. I backed away, preparing for her to swing on me but got a giggle instead.

Huh?

"Relax, Asha. I'm not coming to murder him."

I got closer to her ear so nobody could hear me. "What the fuck is going on with you? I don't think I need to tell you how stupid it would be to kill the Jamaican man with dozens of snipers who, by the way, just held you hostage for almost a week."

"Relax, Asha. I won't do anything crazy."

I stood upright and fixed my dress. "Okay."

After the other members arrived, we all walked inside and sat in the largest VIP section on the second floor. It was the only section that would fit us all. Since our members also brought friends with them, we were at least thirty people deep.

After getting a few drinks in my system, I split from the gang. They all understood why. I couldn't be seen by anyone partying with one of the most lethal group of women in Dallas.

Once I got to the bar, I kept an eye on the door and the entrance to the section where my girls were. I always watched their backs when I ducked off the scene. It was the least I could do. "Long Island Iced Tea on the house for the beautiful lady," I heard a voice say above me.

Swiftly turning my head, I saw it was Delyle. He smelled soft and fresh—heavenly. "You scared me."

He sat next to me and pulled the stool closer. "Don't be. How's everything going?"

Exhaling, I took a sip of the drink. "Actually, pretty good. It was Sway's idea to come here tonight."

"I'm sure." He grinned, looking up at the second floor. Sway was standing by the railing with a drink in her hand, eyes glued on Delyle.

"If you don't mind me asking, what did you do to her?"

"I don't think I understand." He and Sway never broke eye contact.

"She's different. You know? We found out someone stole from us recently, and she didn't do what Sway would do."

"You mean she didn't kill that person."

"Exactly."

He nodded up at her in approval. "She's learning."

"Learning what?"

"I didn't harm your friend in any way. If that's what you're asking."

"You promise?"

"I don't have to promise. I gave you my word. I don't say things I don't mean, and I've never broken my word."

"Okay."

He ordered me one more drink on the house and made his way to the second floor where Sway was. She tried to hide her excitement, but I could see it from where I sat. This wasn't like her. No man other than Houston ever made her blush. She was tough and hard to reach at times. But Delyle seemed to do it with ease. For the life of me, I couldn't make the situation make sense. He broke all the rules.

After taking my second drink, I made my rounds, speaking to people I knew. A few officers were in the building, including Dennis. I tried to walk past him, but he caught up to me.

I rolled my eyes. "Dennis, don't do this. Act like we're at work."

Dennis and I were once in a relationship, but like any other man, he couldn't keep his dick to himself. We were very good at keeping things cordial in the workplace environment, but anytime he saw me out, things changed. "Can we talk? I've done everything you've asked of me. I just want to talk."

Finally, I allowed him to lure me into a small corner of the club so we could be alone. "Yes?"

He looked as if he had so much to say before, but the words had escaped him. "You look gorgeous."

"Thanks."

"You came alone?"

"I go everywhere alone," I lied. The goons were always around.

"The club is nice. He really put it together." I smacked my lips and attempted to walk away, but he gently pulled me back.

"Please, don't leave."

"Then say what you want to say."

"I love you, Asha. I love everything about you. I don't think I can do this life thing without you. Moms still asking about you. Pops calling me stupid. I don't know what to do."

Just as I was about to respond, an arm was tossed over Dennis' shoulder. "This nigga over here being a gnat again," Demaris said.

Demaris was Dennis' younger brother—younger by a year. They had the same mom and same dad but were still so different. Demaris was a darker version of his brother. He'd done some time in prison, so he was strong and buff. He was taller than Dennis and lankier but still had a great body. His hair was wavy, and he rocked diamonds in his mouth that glistened in the dark. It looked good on him. Demaris had these cold eyes about him that gave me the chills.

"Mind your business, nigga. Every time you see me trying to get my girl back, you come cock blocking." Dennis would've been red right now if he was white. He was heated. It was true, though. Demaris always had to put his two cents in. The two obviously didn't get along.

"Stop begging, and maybe your hoe will take you back."

Before Dennis could swing on Demaris, I stood in the middle. "Demaris, knock it off."

He gave me the once over and winked at me. "You right. I'll leave. Wouldn't want to disrupt anyone's peace." He pulled at his sagging jeans and walked away while chugging on some beer.

Dennis dusted the wrinkles from him. "It's all good, Dennis. Look, how about this, you go home, and I'll come by later. Okay? And we can talk."

He looked like a sad dog and put his head down. "Okay, Asha. Please come. I'll be waiting for you."

"I will." I rubbed his back and walked away.

I loved Dennis but also hated him. He was the type of man who would cry and beg but still waste a woman's time. If he wasn't so much of a dog, I would've given him a chance long ago. The problem was, we'd been there far too many times to count.

Dennis was well known for being the sexy cop in Dallas. He'd gone viral online many times and had over a million followers on Instagram. People would stop and take pictures with him whenever they saw him, and the woman threw themselves at him. Just because he was a cop didn't mean he was perfect. Just like any other no-good negro, he took the bait. To push the bar even further, he'd funded quite a few abortions. Being that he was fertile, I made sure to never stray away from my birth control.

Just like I knew it would, after a while, being at the club started to bore me. Don't get me wrong, the music was bumping, and the drinks were good and potent—I just didn't have the energy. Part of me wanted to be home, watching *Cold Case Files* on Netflix. I'd grown to like being alone. A lot of things were getting old to me.

Just recently, I'd been talking to human resources about becoming a homicide detective. They told me everything I needed in order to make sure that happened for me. Being a detective had always been a fantasy of mine, and it just fell into my life. I originally took this path because I wanted to be a cop and make sure the gang was good. I had forgotten all about my childhood dreams of solving horrific murders. It was crazy how no matter what path I took and why, it still led me straight to my dreams.

After getting over Dennis, I had a lot of time to myself, so that was plenty of time to think. I became obsessed with making myself a better person. It was so much going on, and though the gang was behind some of it, I could vouch that we didn't bother anyone until they bothered us except for Sway. Lately, she'd been bothering everyone. She didn't give a damn who it was.

As I walked toward the ladies' room, I nodded up at Spin, letting her know I would be making my exit soon. She nodded back and popped another bottle. Knowing Spin, she would be leaving soon, too, so she could lay up with Terry. Never failed.

The long hallway down to the restroom was empty and quiet. The sound of my heels echoed against the floor. Suddenly, I stopped and froze. Being a cop, mixed with being from the streets, I had a heightened sixth sense. I felt the presence of someone behind me. Instinctively, I reached for my gun, which I did not have, and tossed my back against the nearest wall.

There was nobody there, but it didn't take the unsettled feeling away. Reluctantly, I started walking toward the ladies' room but faster. The closer I got, the faster I walked. It was right next to the back exit door.

The second my hand touched the silver handle to the ladies' room, I felt cold steel pressed against the back of my neck. I couldn't see who it was, but I had an idea.

"What do you want?"

"Go out the back door."

"Okay. Just calm down."

"I am calm," he said, sounding everything but calm. The gun was now pressed into my back.

Doing as I was told, I grabbed my purse and pushed the back door open. When an alarm didn't go off, I sighed. Usually, back doors to large establishments had loud, obnoxious alarms when the door was touched.

Inside my purse, I always kept three large bottles of perfume and mace. Not because I wanted to smell like three different perfumes, but because in situations like this, when I couldn't carry a gun, the purse was my weapon.

As he slowly walked me to the dumpster, I heard muffled music from the club and crickets. The light on the pole flickered on and off, making it look like a strobe light.

He finally jerked me around, and there I was, standing face to face with Damaris. I knew it. "Before you do anything crazy, think about who you're dealing with."

He cocked the gun, not letting it leave my forehead. His eyes glossed. He acted so tough, but I knew his soft spot. I knew because it was me. "Why is Dennis on his way home to wait for you?"

"I told him to."

He pushed me back against the dumpster. A raccoon and its babies ran from under the dumpster and in the opposite direction. "Why do you fucking insist on playing these types of games with me? Bitch, you know I ain't stable."

Demaris and I had sex three times while I was getting over my heartbreak from Dennis. Demaris was there for me in more ways than one. I thought he was misunderstood at first, the black sheep even. It didn't take long for me to see that Demaris was exactly what they said he was—a menace. He pretended just to get me, and once he got me, he was worse than his brother.

"You comforted me and took advantage when I was vulnerable. You used my depression to fuck me, and you want to sit here with a gun to my face because I didn't completely fall for it?"

"Bitch, I love you!"

"No, you don't. You're infatuated with something you can't have. That's all. Move on. You have plenty of women at your beck and call. Gravitate toward them. What we had is over."

"You don't mean that."

I took in a deep breath. I wouldn't need my weapon. We'd been there before. At that point, I was annoyed. All I wanted was for him and his brother to leave me alone.

As I was wondering how to get him away from me, a van came screeching around the corner and down the alley toward us. Three masked men jumped out and drew guns on me.

Demaris held up his hands and shook his head. "Nevermind, fam. I was tripping," he said to the men.

They nodded at him, got back in the van, and drove away. I

couldn't breathe. My vision had blurred, and my legs had locked. "What the fuck?"

He tucked his gun. "I'm so sorry. I lost my cool and almost did some dumb shit."

I finally caught my breath and dropped my purse. "Demaris, did you put a hit on me?"

He nodded and grabbed the bridge of his nose. "You don't understand how much I love you, Asha."

I pointed in the direction the van went. "That's not fucking love! That was obsessive! That was crazy!"

"And now it's gone." He tried to grab my arm, but I pushed him away. "I fucked up. I know. I don't know what's going on in my head."

I backed against the dumpster even more and grabbed my chest. In just a few short moments, my life was almost gone. This man was crazy. "You have a problem."

"My only problem is you. You so quick to give up on everything, Asha, everything. I wasn't playing around when I said I love you, my nigga. I really love your goofy ass. I still remember everything you told me. Shit, I remember everything I told you. I remember how good it feels to be inside of you. My only flaw is what? I'm a lil' possessive? Grow up."

He shook his head and let out a small breath. "You don't give me space. This right here just proves it. What about your brother? Huh? Have you thought about him? He's going to be devastated."

"We don't have to tell him just yet." He looked as if he had something to say on the tip of his tongue, but it wouldn't come out. Instead, he settled for asking, "What you see in my brother that you don't see in me? Tell me that."

"I don't know."

"Is it 'cause I'm a gangsta and he not? You think that makes him better? I would never do you how he did you."

"Yeah, you'll just get me killed instead. Right, gotcha."

He smashed his fist against the dumpster, leaving a huge dent.

That three-year bid he did in prison really put some strength on him.

"I want you so bad."

"Bad enough to kill me?"

He half smiled. Not because he was happy but because he didn't know what else to say. "Look, if you do go over tonight, make sure you use protection."

"My sex life is none of your business, but why would you request that?"

"You've been taking aspirin, not birth control. He switched it out when you weren't home the other day. The law is giving women a hard time with abortions these days, so I just wanted you to be careful."

"How do you know?"

"He told my mom, and she's been struggling with if she should tell you or not. So, she told me, and I made the decision to tell you." He backed away and walked back to the exit door.

"Demaris!"

"Yo?"

"How'd you get a gun into the club?"

"My dad and Delyle were very close. He let me bring it inside off the strength of that."

"So, he let a hot head bring a gun because he knew your dead father? No. Tell me the truth." I wasn't satisfied with that answer.

He looked down at his shoes and smiled. Then he looked back up at me. "Tell Sway no need to say thank you. Laytron was a bitch anyway. His body will never be found. He had it coming."

With that, he walked away.

SWAY
THE TOP FLOOR

He greeted me so smoothly that it was almost as if he didn't have me in his dungeon for three days. He approached me like we'd been old pals who were simply being reacquainted.

"Nice to see you again. May I have a seat?" he asked, tugging on his suit.

I shrugged. "It's your club."

"True." He checked to make sure the seat was clean and sat down right across from me. The gang was far too busy enjoying themselves to realize I was now right in front of the man who had me tied up below his home. "How are you liking it?"

"It's very nice. You pulled it off so clean, considering it was a hold on the opening."

"Thanks to you."

"You're very welcome," I said. Looking around, I asked, "Is there some sick dungeon here, too?"

"Yes."

"What?"

"Yes, but it's not below the club. It's on the top floor."

"The second floor?"

"The third."

"I thought it was only two floors."

"Do you want to see it?"

"Fuck no." I shook my head. "You called me disgusting. Even if it was to describe a feeling, it was used to define a feeling toward me."

"Your actions provoked my criticism."

"What about your actions?"

"I helped you."

"You kidnapped me!" At the realization that I was losing my cool, I calmed down and glanced around to ensure no one heard me.

His jaws clenched as he stood up. "It's a janitor's closet. Open it and go through the double doors, then take the elevator to the third floor. Don't worry about the code. I'll see you and buzz you up."

"I'm not coming."

"Yes, you will." He walked away with pure confidence and anger. My tone offended him deeply, and I could tell. I did it purposely.

I looked to the left just in time to catch Spin pretending not to look at me.

Way up at the top of the club, I saw a darkly tinted glass that stretched feet across. It would come off as a decoration if he hadn't just told me it was a third floor. To willingly walk into another closed in space when he had just let me go from one would be insane.

For another twenty minutes or so, I listened to music and zoned completely out. The more I drank, the greater the force grew in my limbs to walk toward the back and into that janitor's closet.

I had to go. I needed to know how far this could go and what it all meant. Maybe I could learn from him. Maybe I needed to get on my damn feet and make my way to that janitor's closet.

"Fuck it." I tossed back another shot and grabbed my clutch.

"Leaving?" Spin asked, grabbing my elbow.

"Just going to the first floor and mingle. Might have the DJ play a few songs."

She didn't look convinced, but she was satisfied enough to nod and let me walk away in peace.

Once I walked down to the first floor, my eyes were trained on the long hallway as thoughts raced through my head. I had to be crazy. Just then, I saw Demaris come from the back exit door. His head seemed to be in the clouds of hell; he was upset. So upset that he didn't even see me coming and bumped right into me.

"My bad, Sway." He grabbed me to keep me from tripping over my own feet.

"It's fine."

I allowed him to fix me. Our eyes locked, and I saw it—he was sad, not angry. He looked as if he was fighting back tears. This was a shock to me because Demaris was more ruthless than I was... way more ruthless. What could possibly have him on the verge of tears?

The back door came swinging open again, but this time, it was Asha. Demaris pulling away from me turned my attention back to him. He gazed at her like he craved her but couldn't have her. I could almost feel his longing.

"Take care, Sway." He walked away and didn't look back.

"What was that about?" I asked once Asha was close enough to me.

"He wants me back." She appeared more emotional than he was.

"You don't want to?" I asked. Asha knew things about me that I didn't tell anyone and vice versa.

"I don't know what to do. I'm just going to Uber home."

"You sure?" I asked.

"I'm sure." Her voice cracked. She slapped her hand over her mouth, so I wouldn't see her crying and ran quickly toward the front door.

Not putting too much thought into them, I focused back on the task at hand. I stood in front of the janitor's closet. I tugged at the door and noticed it was locked. There was a box for a code that I didn't have. That's when I heard the *clink* noise. Soon as I opened the door and walked inside, it closed behind me on its own.

The double doors were to the left, which had another code. The doors opened again without me touching the code box.

Behind the double doors was a black gate. I pulled it back and stepped onto the spacious elevator. I pressed the number three for the top floor. It took a few moments, longer than I expected it to take.

Once at the top, I was face to face with Delyle. He opened the gate and stepped to the side. "You're stubborn. I don't like it," he said as I walked past him.

"So, what's up?" I asked, peering around the spacious loft.

It was the size of the entire jewelry section at JC Penny. The black marble floors went perfectly with the black walls. He had a kitchen, a bedroom area, and an area full of sex toys and machinery. There were other things I saw but didn't quite understand what I was looking at. For example, there was a doll sprawled out on the floor. She looked so real.

He saw my face and nodded. "She's real."

"Bullshit."

"Veronica," he called out.

The woman, who looked nearly identical to a Tyra Banks life-sized doll, stood to her feet and removed the eye mask. "Yes, Daddy?"

"Make the pretty lady a drink. Please?"

She nodded and winked at him. "No problem, Daddy." She smiled at me and walked to the other side of the loft to the kitchen.

"Have a seat," he said.

I didn't move. He liked to be in control, and so did I. Once he saw I didn't move, he didn't get upset. In fact, he gave me a pleasant smile. "Veronica?"

"Yes, Daddy?"

"Never mind on the drink. Take the pretty lady back down the stairs. I'll wait here for you."

"Wait," I said as I watched her walk over to me. "What are you doing?"

"I don't have the time nor the patience to deal with defiance."

"You're the one who invited me up."

"And now I'm inviting you to leave." He glanced at Veronica. "Use force if she gives you any issues. I have a call." He walked away and answered his ringing cellular device.

I pulled away from her, and just like that, the sweet woman flipped me and body slammed me with ease. She was so small but deadly and strong. Her elbow was in my neck, making it hard to breathe.

"I want to stay! Please!" I yelled the best I could so Delyle could hear me.

He hung up the call and slowly walked over to us, looking down at me. "What was that?"

"I want to stay."

He nodded at Veronica. "Help the pretty lady up. Finish the drink. Let's make her comfortable."

Just like a robot, Veronica was back to being sweet and passive. She helped me up and apologized for assaulting me. Of course, I didn't accept her apology, but I didn't have a choice. Something about Delyle demanded my attention and my obedience. I wanted to be in his presence.

"Do you have anything you want to say?" he asked as I tried to take a seat like he initially asked.

"Huh?"

"Your behavior wasn't called for."

"I'm sorry for being so rude. You've been very patient with me. And the least I can do is show some respect," I said and meant it from the bottom of my heart.

He could've killed me in that basement, but he let me live. What I did was unspeakable. I could've brought his entire organization down had he not moved that body. His club would've been under a federal magnifying glass. I had killed for less.

Veronica handed me a drink. "It's a cognac with Coke. I hope you're a cognac drinker." She looked truly nervous as to what I might say back. She aimed to please, and it was clear.

"I love cognac." I smiled and took a sip. Her kindness somehow enticed a kindness inside of me.

"This is a safe place, Katie. We don't need Sway."

I almost fixed my lips to ask how he knew my name but decided against it. "Would you mind if I kissed you?" Veronica asked.

It caught me off guard. My eyes switched from her to Delyle. Almost as if I needed his approval.

"I've never kissed a girl."

I was nervous. If the gang knew I was on this third floor acting like a little bitch, they would be so ashamed. My street credit didn't matter up there. I had no gun. Yes, I could've gone toe to toe with Veronica, but I was far too tipsy and wanted Delyle's attention, not his disappointment. Up there on the top floor, I was Katie Vermont.

"Do you want to try?" she asked.

Again, I glanced at Delyle. "All you have to do is say yes, and she'll take it from there. Say no, and she'll never ask again."

Veronica agreed by nodding.

"Yes," I said.

Just like he promised, she took control.

She got closer to me and gazed deeply into my eyes. "Relax," she whispered and kissed me softly. "How did that feel?"

"Amazing." I kissed her just how she'd just kissed me.

Before I knew it, she was between my legs and watching me as she pleased my pussy with her silky tongue. My hands grabbed my breasts, and my back arched. "Yes," I moaned.

I couldn't believe I was actually having a lesbian experience with a woman who was introduced to me by the man who kidnapped me.

Delyle walked over with a drink in one hand, using the other to massage my head. He smirked as if he knew I was in heaven. Just as I tugged him near me, he walked away and stood by the glass wall that overlooked the entire club.

"Daddy made me earn his affection. You shall, too." That was the last thing I remembered before Veronica carried me off into the clouds.

Asha
Risky Business

I usually like to keep my word. Even though Demaris had just told me about his brother replacing my birth control, I was still on my way to Dennis' apartment. We needed to talk now more than ever. For one, I needed to know why he had a copy of the spare key. He gave it back, but I should've known he would've gotten a spare made. He was a cop, just like I was. Having a plan B was in our nature.

He would spend the first thirty minutes attempting to make love, so that meant the first half hour would consist of me telling him I didn't come there for sex. My eyes rolled at how I put my foot in my mouth when I promised to come over after the club.

Just as the Uber neared his apartment, I got a call from Dennis. "I'm almost there."

I heard the wind and keys in his background. It sounded like he was running. "Hey, can we do this another time? They just called me in to work. There was a murder outside the police station."

"Do they need me, too?"

"I don't believe so. They called me because one of the cops killed was the one who had my shift for today."

"Ouch. They know who did it?"

"Nah, that's what they're doing now. It's a manhunt for that area."

"Okay. Just call me when you can."

"Bet." He hung up.

This was spooky because I lived near the police station, which was downtown.

"Is it too late to reroute?" I asked the Uber driver.

His eyes roamed up to the rearview mirror.

"No, ma'am. I will pull over, so you can just edit the location. Is it far from where you were going initially?"

"No, sir. It's fairly close."

He nodded and waited. To be honest, I was a little disappointed that I couldn't see Dennis. I wanted so badly to look him in his eyes and ask him why he would do something so downright crazy. I wanted to see what he would say.

Maybe it was good I couldn't confront him because then he would ask me how I knew. It would start something between him and Demaris.

On the way home, I snagged some food from a wing spot and a bottle of wine from the store near my house. The owner knew me and would sell liquor at any time. Even if it was after hours.

Shock still consumed me about Demaris almost having me kidnapped less than thirty minutes ago. What was going to happen to me? How fast did he call the hit after he heard about me going to spend time with his brother? Most importantly, he had me wondering the difference between love and obsession. Did he love me, or was he obsessed with me? Could I be with a man like him? We both were in the streets, but he was in the streets heavy. Just like Sway, he'd been behind a great deal of the shootings in the city. He didn't care about much, so why would I believe he cared about me?

Those are things I wanted to ask him. Now, I never would. I didn't want to get on Demaris' bad side. His love scared me. Maybe his obsession scared me.

We finally made it to my apartment. I gave the driver a tip in cash and on the app. "I know the app takes money away from your tip, so here you go," I said when I stepped out and handed him a hundred-dollar bill.

He was thankful. He even asked me if I wanted to stop at a store before going inside.

My apartment complex was luxurious and secured. It wasn't easy getting inside unless one had the code or was an expert at breaking into highly secured places. Security was never an issue for me.

Once I made it through the many coded gates and into my breezeway, I got a buzz on the phone but was too occupied with finding my keys to check and see who it was from.

After searching for my apartment key and walking inside, a strong force stopped me from closing the door. I would've been frightened, but I saw a familiar face with his foot blocking me from closing my door.

"Demaris? What the fuck?"

He didn't look alarmed, just hurt as he was when I saw him last. "Let me in."

"Go home."

At last, he forced his way inside and locked the door behind him. No longer did he smell like fresh cologne. He reeked of fresh blood. It was just now that I started to realize he was soaked in red blood. I was more worried than he was. With one hand, I snatched him further inside and locked the door.

"Are you crazy?" I asked as I locked the door.

"It wasn't supposed to happen like this, mama. I just wanted to see you tonight." He walked over to the large window and glanced down at the city.

I placed the things in my hand on the counter, keeping my eyes on him. "What do you mean? And whose blood is this?"

"The cop whose face is splattered all over the news." With much ease, he spoke of something so detrimental

"Stop playing."

He twisted his head, not his body, to look at me. "He took the shift of my brother. I came here tonight to see you, and here he comes pulling me over." He must have seen the disappointed look on my face because he came over and grabbed my hands. "Don't look at me like that. He knew who I was when he stopped me, Asha. He then attempted to extort me. Why you even looking at me like that? Huh? What about him?"

I tried not to get emotional, but I did. Demaris looked so vulnerable at that moment. No longer was he a tough guy with bodies under his belt. He was my teddy bear like he'd been so many times before.

"You killed him?" I stepped back and grabbed my head. "You're not serious."

"Can you bleach these clothes for me? Maybe let me shower?"

"So, you're really being truthful right now?" I still couldn't believe it.

"I wouldn't waste my time lying to you. I have a manhunt out there just itching to catch me with these clothes on. Please, Asha." He looked entirely depleted of energy.

Without another thought, I allowed him to shower. I then bleached his clothes and burned them on my balcony in a barbecue pit as he bathed. After the clothes were nothing but mere ashes, I sat on the side of the tub and gazed into his dark eyes. "You know I can get into a lot of trouble for this, right?"

With his eyes half closed, he said, "Trust me, I know. I would go to jail for a thousand years before I let you get caught up in my shit."

Using a brand new sponge, I squeezed warm water onto his head and the rest of his body. I would be lying if I said I didn't gain pleasure from seeing how relaxed he was. Here, he had no reason to keep his guard up, and he knew it.

"What happened?"

"I told you, I was on my way here, and he pulled me over, telling me to pay him or get locked up. I guess today just wasn't his lucky day."

"Does your brother know?"

"Fuck no. The only person who knows I was behind this shit is you."

"What about the men you sent to kidnap me tonight?"

His head turned to me. Still, he looked so content. "Not even they know. Only you."

I nodded. "Your secret is safe with me."

I was a cop, but before all, I was a hood bitch. His secret was indeed safe with me. No matter what.

"They're saying that cop is dead."

"I know he is. I shot him up in the head three times. I don't know why he felt the need to play with me, of all people. It wasn't safe, and he knew that."

I scrubbed some blood from the corner of his lip. "Your brother called me and called off our meeting. The entire city is looking for you. What if they come here?"

He snatched the sponge from me. "I ain't come here because I felt like they wouldn't reach me here. I came because this is where I was on my way to anyway. I wanted to see you no matter what."

I sat in silence for a few moments before I finally spoke. "You don't love me, Demaris. You're obsessed with me. The minute I give you what you want, you'll be gone," I said before I knew it.

He gasped. "You really think that? Don't you?"

"I do."

He grabbed my soft hands. "I'm here because I fucking love you, my nigga. Why can't you see that?"

Shook, I pulled back from him. "How am I supposed to know that?"

I heard the water dripping from him as he stood up with his big dick hanging between his legs. "How you supposed to know that? Let me show you."

He stepped out of the tub, smelling like fresh soap, and grabbed me by my neck. For a second, the only sound was our breathing. After gazing into my eyes for a few moments, he pulled me in for a wet and juicy kiss. My clothes were now drenched because he gave us no space.

"Stop," I whimpered once the grip from his hands on my neck became too much. Instead, his grip tightened.

His jaws clenched, and he looked me dead in my eyes. There was no laughing. No playing bone in his body. "I love you. I need you to love me back, Asha, or I'll go crazy."

"I can't."

With his hand still gripped right around my neck, he forced me through the door and onto my bed. "If you want me to stop, then say it."

I said nothing. Deep down, I wanted him to take me. Him having his entire way with me was all I wanted. He knew it. He always knew.

Demaris snatched my thong off and pulled me toward him by my thick thighs. I knew he was about to punish me, but I still didn't tell him to stop. I wanted this. I needed this. I needed him. For some reason, by gazing into his cold eyes, I felt we needed each other.

His warm member plunged into my wet pussy with no warning. "I need you," he grunted.

I couldn't speak. My words were mere moans. His sex felt so good inside of me like it always had. It almost felt wrong to feel this right. We had a stare down as he took me. The nails in his fingers dug into my ass cheeks as he intensely made love to me.

Knock. Knock.

A sudden guest at the door interrupted us from going further. He pulled his dick out of me as we both caught our breath. His eyes were red, and so were mine. Why was I crying? Did I love him, too?

"Shit," I said as I inhaled and exhaled.

He backed against the wall, stroking his dick, waiting for me to answer the door. "Pass me my robe," I said, eyeing the black silk robe that hung on the door next to him.

He snatched it and tossed it to me. "Hurry up. I still need to talk to you."

"We ain't doing much talking," I said.

"Get the door."

I nodded and walked away with my pussy still throbbing. I was so used to controlling things in my life, but with Demaris, I controlled absolutely nothing. Just like Delyle did for Sway, Demaris broke all the rules. Only difference was that Demaris harbored strong feelings toward me, and he showed it.

Eager to get back to the dick down I was receiving, I snatched the door open. Standing at the door was Dennis with his work clothes on and a notepad. He didn't look surprised. Dennis knew exactly where I lived, so his being there was no mistake.

His mug turned to a smile once he saw me. "I came to ask a few questions. As you may know, there was a shooting just minutes away from you. With surveillance at our disposal, we have reason to believe that a masked man may be in this apartment building or near."

Boy, was I happy his body camera was on. If it wasn't, he would've been inside my home right now, trying to do what his brother had already succeeded in doing tonight—pulling me into my feelings with his dick.

"Oh, no. Well, I don't know anything about that. I just made it home from a club."

He knew I wasn't lying, so this made it even easier. "Have you seen or heard anything suspicious?"

"No, sir."

He handed me a card. "If you hear or see anything suspicious, give the detective on this case a call."

I took the card and tightened my robe. "I will. Thanks for coming by and warning everyone."

He bit his bottom lip and winked at me. "Pleasure is all mine." He turned the other way and pinched my nipple, so the camera wouldn't see it. "Be safe tonight and lock up."

"Will do." I quickly closed the door.

Before going back into the bedroom, I grabbed Demaris a bottle of water to save myself an extra trip. He always asked for a bottle of water after sex.

It was dark in my bedroom, but the light from the kitchen gave me a glimpse of Demaris sitting at the edge of the bed with his monster between his legs, waiting patiently for me. He pulled me between his legs once I got close enough and put the water bottle on the nightstand. He then slid my robe down and bent me over the bed.

With my back arched, and my pussy waiting to be met by his member, I turned to look back at him. "Your body is beautiful. You're beautiful."

I blushed, still on all fours. He always flooded me with compliments. This was how I fell for him the first time. I was starting to think maybe it wasn't a game. Maybe he did love me, just too much.

"Thank you, baby," I said before I knew it.

Instead of penetrating me right away, he got closer to me and rubbed his rock hard dick on my ass. Gently, he pulled me by grabbing the back of my neck. His hot breath tingled on my neck, further enticing me. "It just feels wrong, but it's not," he said, planting warm kisses on the back of my shoulders.

"I know." I was barely thinking straight with him turning me on the way he was.

His hands grabbed my waist as he licked the inside of my earlobe. "Asha?"

His whispering in my ear was enough to make me cum alone. "Yes?"

"You don't love me?"

"I'm not supposed to."

"But do you?"

"Yes."

"Say it," he said, sliding his dick into my moist pussy from behind.

"I love you."

Demaris held onto me so tightly, smothering me with all of him. He used his hand on the back of my neck to guide me back onto the bed. My back naturally arched as he gave me deep, hard strokes. "Say it again."

"I love you."

"Say it like you mean it."

"I love you, baby."

"Do you really?" Instead of responding, I moaned out in pure satisfaction. He pressed deeper into me. "I asked a question."

"Yes, I really love you."

"You really, really love me?" He pounded harder and grabbed tighter like he was reaching his climax.

My head turned back to him. "I really, really love you."

Hearing me say it again sent him over the edge, pushing him to release. He pulled out, his dick making a plopping noise, and held it so the cum wouldn't fall onto my floor.

"Fuck." His breath was rapid but deep. "That pussy do something to me." He slightly laughed.

My hands let go, and I plopped onto the bed.

After we both washed up, I made his favorite snack after sex: tacos. After eating, we brushed our teeth and cuddled in bed while watching a horror movie on Hulu.

My leg was wrapped around him as he lay on his back, smoking a blunt. "You doing a good job keeping your affiliation with the Spindarellas under the radar, but be careful."

"What you mean?"

"You sat with them for a while before you moved at the club. It wasn't long enough to really raise suspicion with the city, but it was enough for Dennis to take notice and ask me about it."

"What did he say?"

"He asked if I had ever seen you with any of the girls."

"What you tell him?"

"What you mean what I tell him?" He looked as if he was annoyed by such a rhetorical question. "I told him he had to be smoking crack to even ask that."

"Thanks, Demaris. You really do look out for me and my best interest."

"But what?"

"I think you might love me too much."

"How could you even say that? You don't want all of me? You want me to treat you like I treat the rest of these hoes?"

"Don't talk to me like that."

"I'm just saying. You don't even think before you talk."

"You like my pussy a lot, and maybe it confused you." I wasn't serious, but I did want to see his reaction.

"The pussy fire. I ain't gon' lie about that." He blew more smoke out of his mouth. "But that's just the cherry on top. It's a whole sundae of reasons why I love you. You want better, and you make me want better. You keep an open mind for almost anything. Bruh, you the first person in my life that ain't ever judged me for who I am. You trusted a gangsta with the most vulnerable parts of you, and I'll never forget that. That shit was risky."

I smiled and kissed him. "A very risky business."

"Hold up." He reached over and grabbed something from his wallet. He then leaned back up and handed it to me. It was a picture of me when I was a teenager. Sway and I were standing outside the projects with Spin and Tweety. "He took this from your nightstand when he switched the birth control. He's been trying to find pictures of Spin and 'em when they were kids to compare to this picture."

I grabbed it and stuffed it under my pillow. "What does he want to do with it?"

"I have no clue. I asked him what would happen if he confirmed his suspicion. He didn't respond."

"Would he actually turn me in?"

"I doubt it."

"That's scary. What if he put cameras in here?"

"He didn't. Trust me. If you don't trust it, then we could always do a sweep."

"It's all good. I'll just keep an extra eye out."

CRYSTAL
I Needed Love Today

My feet ached horribly, leaving me to collapse on the couch as soon as I opened the door to my home. I barely even made it past the coffee table. Usually, I would turn some '90s R&B on and relax with some wine until I fell asleep, but that's not what my body had in mind. I completely shut down.

Even early in the morning, it was blistering hot outside. Working the night shift definitely had its perks because leaving for work wasn't as hot. I loved the night shift.

Just as my eyes were closing, my phone rang. It was my sister-in-law, Tenise. She probably just wanted to vent to me about my older brother, her husband, so I declined. We would talk when I woke up.

As I was dozing off again, she called back. Frustrated, I snatched the phone to my ear and let it rest on my cheek. "Yes?"

"Hey." I heard her sniffling and crying. She tried to act as if she wasn't, but the long pauses were so telling.

"What's wrong, Te?" I sighed.

"Have you seen the news?"

When she asked that, I was immediately awake. It's like

someone had instantly slapped me wide awake. I just knew something was wrong. "Why?"

"Please, just do it, sis. I don't even have the heart to say it to you."

"Where's my brother? Is he home from his shift?" I asked, scared to turn the TV on. He worked as a police officer on the night shift over in Dallas.

"Turn the news on, Crystal." She hung up the phone soon as my niece started to cry.

I turned the TV onto Fox 4 news and sat back. At first, all I could see was the helicopter flying over the police scene. Then my brain directed me to the downtown scenery. And then I saw it; the caption on the screen read: ***Police Officer Fatally Shot.***

Jumping to my feet, I called my sister-in-law back. Those two rings it took for her to answer the phone felt like two hours. "It was him, Crystal. And yes, I'm sure. I identified the body this morning."

This time, I was the one who ended the call. I couldn't take it. I couldn't take anything. It was like I physically felt my heart break down into tiny pieces. Some pieces I knew I could never get back.

How could this happen? My brother didn't bother anyone. He was the sweetest man I'd ever known. As kids and even on into adulthood, he'd never had one confrontation.

As I aimlessly roamed around the house, I still heard the TV going. As of now, there were no suspects, but a man in a hoodie was seen running under a bridge. That gave little to no explanation at all. That sounded like every homeless person downtown.

The sun hadn't yet risen when I made it home, but now it was up. I hadn't noticed the time quickly passing by. Just like I didn't notice that I had broken my TV, coffee table and kitchen table. The plant on my kitchen island was now scattered around my house.

When I had finally calmed down, I took a look at what I had done—damage. How my home looked is about how I felt inside. I was so torn apart by all of this.

After trying to calm my nerves, I went on another rampage. I didn't know exactly when or how she got in, but Icis was holding me from behind, rocking me back and forth, and grabbing my arms so I couldn't destroy anything else of mine.

"I saw the news, baby. I'm so sorry. I am so sorry. I know how you feel." She rocked me back and forth.

Icis had seen so many bad days that I knew she understood, but that's not what I wanted to hear. I wanted to hear that the news was wrong and my brother wasn't dead. I wanted to hear Terry coming through the door, telling me he got there as fast as he could. I wanted some love today. I needed love today.

Icis held me for hours until I cried myself to sleep.

SWAY

TIWANNA AND THE FISHERMAN

I had been in the shower for an hour, ever since Fray left my apartment. He'd become more and more comfortable doing what he was doing to me. Usually, he would come by on the days I was supposed to have home visits, but it was a Sunday, and he popped up early. He even stayed a little longer and made himself at home by eating leftovers in the fridge. I couldn't do this anymore.

It seemed like I had scrubbed myself raw in the shower. I rubbed and rubbed until I almost had carpet burn. I wanted his stench off of me. Even though I smelled completely of Dove soap and body wash, I could still smell him. It was all in my head, and that was a problem.

After showering, I walked into Spin's room to see if she was home, and she wasn't. For the last five days, she had hardly been home. It had me worried, but now I didn't have the time to worry. There was another point on my agenda to hit today. I couldn't keep feeling like this.

I knew just who to call, but I didn't have his number. All I knew was how to get back to his home, which was over an hour away on the outskirts of the city.

After getting dressed, there was plenty of time for a hefty

breakfast, but I had no appetite. The smell of Fray's breath freshly made me nauseated. I hated him.

On the way to Delyle's home, I thought about everything that could go wrong. Though we didn't sleep with each other, and he only watched, I still felt there was some sort of intimacy. As his eyes examined me that night, I felt the connection. Maybe he did this with everyone. I didn't know—all I knew was I needed his help with a problem I was currently dealing with, and I was willing to face his rejection just for the chance that he may help. I was desperate for his help.

Once at his estate, I shocked myself to see that I actually remembered how to get back there. It was pretty easy once I passed two counties and the highways got thinner.

To my surprise, there wasn't a heap of vehicles or security when I pulled up. In fact, there were no cars down the long driveway that led to his home. That didn't make me nervous, but then again, I didn't want to come out there for nothing.

Once I got out of the car, I fixed my half top and booty cutter shorts. I swung my dreads out of my face, grabbing them with my long nails and watching nervously. That's when I saw the front door open. He stood there with a white dish rag thrown over his shoulder and a pot in his hand.

"Come in."

"What?"

I was shocked, to say the least. He didn't seem upset. I just knew I would get some sort of backlash for popping up on him, given our history.

"You didn't drive all this way to sit outdoors? Did you?"

His body looked so perfect. I instantly started to wonder who else had been blessed enough to have felt him inside of them. I wanted to know how it felt inside of me. Was he gentle? Was it rough? Was he caring? Or was he just the type to get a nut and leave a bitch?

Na, he's way too complex for that.

As I walked past him, he took a spoon and slowly put it to my mouth. I stopped, looking confused. "Taste it."

I opened my mouth and accepted the red sauce. It was spicy and sweet. "What's this?"

"Sauce for the oxtails. What do you think? Be honest." He closed the door behind us and led me to the large kitchen. He then pulled a chair out for me at the island.

"It's delicious. I'm not surprised you can cook."

"Why is that?"

"You seem like a man of many, many talents. Making a girl feel special after holding her captive for three days isn't something most men can pull off, I suppose."

"Hungry?" he asked.

"It's funny you ask."

"What's so funny?" He was already setting a plate in front of me.

"I didn't eat at all today."

Delyle switched pots and used a large spoon to lay three meaty oxtails with sauce in front of me. He added cabbage and rice and beans on the other side. He then held up two bottles of wine. One red and one white. "White," I said.

"I figured. Red seems to be loaded with sugars, but it gets the job done."

"Not really a wine type of girl, so I wouldn't know."

"I can teach you."

"Why do I need to know about wine?"

"Unless you want to be back in the ghetto all your life, I suggest you rapidly expand your taste. You'd be surprised how much networking goes on at a simple wine tasting." He nodded at the complete meal laid in front of me. "Eat while you explain to me what was so important that you drove over an hour to my home."

One bite of my food, and I began to see a life with this man. I shook it off but not fast enough. He caught the grin. "Never had food like that, huh?"

"Never."

"Don't get used to it. I don't do it often."

"What made you do it today."

"I had time to spare." He sat across from me and poured a small glass of wine. "You came later than expected."

"Meaning?"

"I expected your presence days ago. I like it."

I continued to eat. I didn't understand how drained I was until I had food in my system. Suddenly, I felt perfectly fine. The sip of wine was the icing on the cake. Though he sat watching, his gestures were so telling. He wasn't upset to see me. He was actually just as anxious as I was.

"I've found myself in need of your help." I barely said it, but I got it out. "And no, I don't need money."

He slightly laughed. "I know it's not money."

"How do you know?"

He leaned over and touched my neck. "It's purple. Someone sucked on your neck so hard that they left the marks of their teeth. I also see bruising on your thighs." I leaned back and tried to hide myself. "Your skin complexion is brighter than others. It was obvious. Who is he?"

"He's my probation officer. I know you won't believe me, nobody will, but he rapes me. And it's becoming more and more frequent. If he ends up dead, the judge already told me she will bring me under federal investigation."

Delyle nodded and sat back in the chair. "I see. You want it to stop but don't know how. What makes you think I have the answers?"

I slid the plate to the side and drank more wine. "While in your basement, you told me there were things worse than death. Your driver told me the same thing in so many words. I need to know what those things are."

"You know what I like about you?"

"What?" I questioned.

"You're willing to learn, and you're willing to learn any way you can. As long as you learn."

"I am. I might be a little desperate, too."

"Desperate is fine. Moving irrationally is not." He stood and took a bowl full of oxtails and tossed them out into the backyard. Just as he closed the door, several large dogs rushed and ate the savory goodness.

"Those are huge. What are they?"

"Cane Corsos." He sat back down. "I want to tell you about this little girl name Tiwanna."

"Okay. I'm listening."

"I would wake up every summer morning on the island I'm from and go play in the river. Mostly to play, but I also caught fish to feed my family. This little girl named Tiwanna would always meet me there along with this man who would also be fishing named Jeff. This went on for about a year. One day, I walked to the river, and not only was Tiwanna not there, but neither was the fisherman. I thought nothing of it. After catching a good amount of fish, I ran back home to drop it off and then went to Tiwanna's house to check on her. Her mother immediately panicked because she thought Tiwanna was with me. Days later, Tiwanna popped back up, but she wasn't the same."

I was almost scared to hear the rest. "This real?"

"Very much so."

"Damn."

"The fisherman had brutally raped her, leaving her to get stitches. He beat her up pretty bad. The fisherman was well liked by the police, so they did nothing. He was a psychopath and helped them take care of hard to deal with fugitives. He killed them. Being that the man was coo-coo, killing him would've been too easy. Getting him arrested was virtually impossible. So, Tiwanna's dad went to see the fisherman one night and fully emasculated him, removing his penis and testicles. Being that the fisherman was known to rape boys and girls often, we knew where his evil was held. So, it was taken away."

"Ouch. What happened to him?"

"He went on for a few more years, but he was forever changed. His pride was gone. His dignity and self-confidence were depleted. He died inside because without the thing he used most to inflict pain, he was nothing more than a dead man walking. Tiwanna's dad didn't have to kill the fisherman, know why?"

"Why?"

"He killed himself." He took my empty plate and tossed the bones to the dogs. "The goal in this lifetime is to get the least blood as possible on your hands while still being a monster."

I sat and thought about what he said. It made sense, and it opened my mind. Never had I thought of anything other than completely eliminating my opposition. "What about the ones who have to be killed?"

"You need to develop discernment to know the difference. Aren't you glad I didn't just eliminate you? You have to know what and who you're dealing with."

"But how do I know?"

"The first ten minutes of talking to someone should tell you any and everything you need to know. Ask the right questions."

"I don't know what I'm dealing with."

"He's a man who uses his power to rape. He's a coward. He doesn't have to be killed. You just kill his demon that he's fighting for him."

CRYSTAL
DEAD TO ME

After my brother's funeral, I went home to cook. When I arrived home, I realized I didn't have all I needed to cook the fish and salad, so I went to the grocery store down the street. I didn't have the energy to do much of anything, but I knew if I didn't get it done right then, I wouldn't get it done.

The day was sunny, as was most Texas summers. Rain would've been great for multiple reasons. I just wanted to loaf, eat, and drink Tequila while listening to the rain, but for now, these blackout curtains would have to work.

After grabbing my shopping cart, I pulled out my phone to reactivate my social media account. My page had been flooded with memorials of my brother on the day of his death, so to cut all that out, I temporarily removed all social media accounts, so I wouldn't see anything that would trigger me. Now, more than ever, I needed Terry. When I needed him during our relationship, he was always there for me. He would come running and kicking doors down just to make sure I was okay, and I missed that about him.

I went to his social media, and just like I expected, there was nothing but old pictures from ten years ago that he had yet to change. Terry was the type to not take social media seriously. Though he still checked Facebook from time to time, looking at his page, you would think he ain't been on there in over a decade. He was such a guy. Guys didn't care about a social image, not real guys anyway. Terry was definitely one of the real ones. He'd had his share of fuck-nigga-shit that he'd done, but it didn't take away from who he was.

As I strolled the aisles, dropping things into the rolling cart, I stumbled upon his girlfriend's page. Spin didn't post much either, but she posted more than Terry. She never posted him on her page. Why? I didn't know yet. But, I saw certain things she would say that he always said. One of his favorite terms to lift his family and friends was, *it's always gon' be another mountain.*

She'd said that a few times within the last few weeks, and I knew it was because they'd been spending time together. My heart almost dropped when I saw her snapping pictures on his couch. I even tossed eggs into the cart like a sack of candy. Luckily, I didn't break anything.

So, this was real. They were really a thing. Just as I was about to get off her page, I noticed something that, for some reason, I'd never noticed before. It was a picture of a handsome young man who'd apparently been shot and killed. She was holding a photo of him at a graveyard. The caption read, *Nobody really knows how we feel. I always thought that you would be here.* There was an emoji of a white dove. After a hashtag, she put R.I.P BRO.

I felt for her. I really did. I'd just lost the most important person in the world to me—my own brother. I could relate.

"They don't have turkey bacon, Terry. Just eat regular bacon today." The sound of my ex-boyfriend's name, who doesn't like regular bacon, coming from a woman's mouth caused me to look up.

"Well, don't get me no bacon," he said on the speaker.

It was him. It was really him. This grocery store was down the street from his place too, so I knew it wasn't a coincidence.

I couldn't believe my eyes. I was staring into the face of the woman whose Facebook page I was now on.

"Hold on, I got a notification," she said. That's when I realized I had accidentally sent her a friend request. Quickly, I canceled it, but it was too late. "Crystal McFrank. McFrank? Isn't that the name of the officer who was just murdered?"

"Hurry up, so you can cook," he said, ignoring her question. Terry loved breakfast for dinner. He still did, I saw.

I trailed behind her but at a safe distance. I wanted to hear him. He sounded so sad whenever he and I talked. It was like he didn't want to. Like he'd rather be doing a million other things than talking to me. To hear him so excited for her to get back to him broke me down on the inside, but all I could do was push the cart and keep quiet.

"I'll get Diamond some treats while I'm here. I saw she was running out."

"Cool. I'm on this game, just hit me when you're outside."

"Okay, baby. I love you."

I could've smashed my cart into her and whooped her ass. I hated her. What did he see in her that he didn't see in me? She was beautiful, and I gave her that, but so was I. I spent years trying to be exactly what I thought he wanted, just for him to fall for the mind of woman he completely despised. If what I heard about her was true, she was into the streets just as hard as he was, and that turned him off completely.

I spent so much time and effort being a woman and not a hood rat. It's like girls like her always won.

I checked out at the same time she did, but I used self-checkout instead.

Once in the car, I drove a few cars in front of her but paid attention. Just like I thought, she turned on Bardin. That was the street to get back to Terry's apartment.

On a day like this, I needed him the most. Not her. He still hadn't called or come over to check on me, and I knew he'd heard about the shooting; he knew my brother was just killed. To see a man I once loved so careless when it came to me felt like grief but for a brand new person.

Once I made it home, I got comfortable and cooked some fried fish and a salad. With Terry on my mind, I could really eat much. Didn't have much of an appetite these days.

Icis had been more of my caregiver than I was hers. When I didn't cook, she came over and cooked for me. When I wasn't feeling my best, it was like she just knew. She came over and made it all better just by listening to me talk about my brother or just listening to me talk, period. She even stayed sober longer and waited until later to get high, just to accommodate my emotional needs.

After a while of TV watching me, I called my brother's phone. I knew it would go to voicemail, but I called anyway and left a message. He couldn't hear it, but it was helping me heal.

"Hey, big bro. The funeral was cool. Just like you joked about as kids, mom had you in a suit with some fresh Jordans on. Everyone came. Even Uncle Elroy came. He was high, but he came. The baby was so sad and blue; it's almost like the baby knew you weren't there. There was no drama, thank God. Mama broke down real bad. Seeing her like that was new to me. It even broke me down. Icis came, and that surprised me because she's been spending a lot of time making sure I'm okay. I know I always said this, but I mean it this time, it's time for me to let the idea of Terry go. It's time for me to let him go completely. I understand that now, and I'm taking the steps starting today."

SWAY
GREMLIN ACTIVATED

It took seven days to get the plan in order, but there I was. I passed the blunt to Ariella as we stared at Fray's home over in Desoto. "You know what to do?" I asked.

She blew out the smoke and passed the blunt back, looking at me like I was crazy. "I'm not a kid anymore, Sway. I got this, trust me." She started checking her pockets.

"What are you looking for?"

"Condoms."

"You ain't need them. It ain't gon' get that far."

She nodded and put her phone in her pocket, but not before calling me. I muted myself. "The code word is golden shower. Correct?"

"Yes," I confirmed. "Make it quick. I want to Uber you home at a decent hour, so Mama Crystal won't be worried."

"You can't drive me home? I thought we just needed a video."

I shook my head. "It's so much more that I need to do with him. I promise you'll be safe."

"I just have a phobia against Ubers. Yeah, I know how to handle my own, but let's not forget, I'm only fourteen. I'm terrified of sex trafficking, and those sickos love teenagers."

"You're right. I'm texting Tweety now. She lives down the street. I'll have her come and take you. Cool?"

She smiled, showing her beautiful dimples. "Cool. I like Tweet."

"Okay."

She got out of the car and walked up the driveway with confidence.

After leaving Delyle's house, I put a plan in motion, all on my own. I needed a teenager who was a far cry from a virgin. My adopted sister, Arielle, was the perfect match. Mama Crystal adopted her when I was still a teenager myself, ten years ago.

Arielle was taken into child protective services at the tender age of four because she was being abused by her uncle. Her mother had died of an overdose when she was three, leaving her in the care of her uncle, who was a sick sadist and couldn't keep his hands to himself. Though he was out of prison for the abuse, he was the only family she had left. For some reason, Arielle still looked out for him when she could. She was the sweetest young lady I'd ever met in my life. She would do anything for Mama Crystal and her adopted siblings.

As I smoked on a blunt, I still couldn't believe how I even let the thought cross my mind to kill Mama Crystal after killing Laytron. Taking away the only good parent Arielle had, all so Mama couldn't talk to the police, was sickening to me. I thought about it often. I needed change. It was time to move differently. Like Delyle told me, I couldn't kill the entire Dallas. It was impossible. And my soul couldn't be as dirty as it was if I wanted to make it past thirty.

I listened as Fray made Arielle a drink. He knew she was fourteen, and he knew she was my sister.

I told Arielle to be waiting at the corner store when he left my house the other day. He always stopped there. I told her to pretend to steal a few items and to make sure Fray saw her. She did. Of course, he pulled her outside after paying for her item and told her to come to his house today or he would turn her in to the police. It was sickening how easily he fell into the wolf trap; so very disappointing.

"You're beautiful, just like your sister. Do you feel good like her?" he asked.

She nervously laughed, but, of course, it was forced. "I hope so. I don't want to get in trouble, Mr. Fray."

"Good. Good. Give me a kiss."

I heard her kiss him. "I'll do anything, sir." He laughed, and I heard his pants unzip. "I'll even do a golden shower."

I tossed the blunt and grabbed the equipment I needed from the back seat. I moved fairly quickly because I didn't want him to go further than he needed to. Not with my little sister or any other girl. It was time to put this sick man into his own walking hell.

"Get on your knees," he said. "I'll put this in the sink." I heard him walk away.

"Hurry up, Sway. Please. He's creepy," she whispered just loud enough so I could hear.

I walked to the back door and attempted to pick the lock, but it was already unlocked. After making sure the volume was on, I started to record. I made it just in time to catch the tip of his dick in Arielle's mouth. She saw me before he did.

Instantly, she started to cry. "Please, Mr. Fray, I'm only fourteen. I don't want to do this. Please. I'm sorry for stealing."

A grin crept across his face as he slammed his dick into her mouth.

"What the fuck is going on here? Arielle, what the hell are you doing?" I asked.

She jumped up and stepped back, looking like a vulnerable teenager. She even had real tears in her eyes, and I made sure to zoom in. Once she walked behind me, so the camera couldn't see her, she smiled.

Fray stood there with his hands up. "You bitch! You dirty bitch! You asked for it! You wanted it!"

I smiled. "Yeah, keep on. Make it all better for us." I turned the camera off and gave it to Arielle just in case Fray tried anything.

Arielle's phone rang. "It's Tweety. She's outside."

I nodded. "Okay. Go straight home. And take this. It's yours." I reached into my pocket and gave her $2,500.

"Sway!" She gave me a big hug and kiss. "You didn't have to."

"But I wanted to. You deserve it."

Tweety blew the horn. "I have to go." She slowly walked away. "Sway?" she said as she stood outside the door.

"Yo."

"I love you."

"I love you, too. Get out of here."

"Okay." She ran away.

Fray stood there frozen with his pants still around his ankles. There was a stool next to him. As I walked to grab it, he tried to charge at me, but I raised my gun. "I wouldn't do that if I were you."

"So what, bitch? Huh? The judge already said if I come up dead, you and your friends will be under federal investigation."

I sat across from him on the stool. "Of course."

It's like he just realized I'd just caught him on camera receiving oral from a minor who indeed cried rape. "You'll never get away with this."

"I will, and this is how it's going to go. You stay my probation officer but no more checks. No more rape. No more drug tests. I do what I want, when I want. You will tell them I am an outstanding woman. You work for me now."

There was a knock at the back door, and I knew exactly who it was. "Come in."

"What's going on? Take your blackmail and leave my home!"

"You thought that's all she wanted?" Veronica asked him with her briefcase.

"Who the hell is this?"

He continued talking shit as Veronica thumbed some fluid in a syringe. He was so upset and deranged that he never noticed the shot go into his neck. He slowly slumped over and fell softly onto the couch.

After Delyle cooked for me and listened to my plans, he told me Veronica was a certified plastic surgeon with over a decade of experience. He gave me her number and told me if I needed her to let her know a few days ahead of time. I called and asked if she knew anything about emasculating male adults, and she did. She'd done several gender changes. But she wouldn't be changing anything, just removing.

Veronica also despised men who abused their power and took advantage of women. She was a strong believer that consenting adults should be the only ones having sex and consenting adults only.

I helped her set the plastic up on the dining table and around it. She also used me to help her set up her utensils and sterilize them. The only hard part was lifting his fat ass onto the table, but we did it.

After shaving and cleaning him, she looked at me over her mask and said, "If you have a weak stomach, I suggest you step aside until it's complete."

"I've seen more things than you can even imagine. Proceed."

She smiled like she liked my come back. "Will do, ma'am."

For the first half of the surgery, I gave her silence to focus. She moved fast with precision. I began to wonder how a woman of her caliber ended up being a crime boss' sex slave.

"I can feel you staring at me," she said as I rested against the wall. She had a mask on, but I still saw a smile in her eyes.

"It's scary how you can turn your crazy on and off at the snap of a finger."

"I only do that for him."

"For Delyle?"

"Yes. Who else, silly?"

"How did he get you like this?"

She shrugged. "My obedience to him was something that

came naturally. I can't explain." She looked over at me. "Can you?"

"Can I what?"

"Can you explain why your obedience to him became natural?"

"Maybe because he had me tied up in a basement."

"I'm aware. I'm the one who gave him the drugs to put you out."

"Good to know," I sarcastically said.

"He's a man of his word. I find it very attractive. I've never quite met anyone like him. If you do exactly as he says, you'll find he's quite addicting and fun."

"How does one even deal with a man like him?"

"He tells you how. All that's required is a listening ear." She giggled and snipped something under the ball sack. "You should be thankful. He rarely steps in like this."

"So, I should be happy that he decided to help me not be sexually abused anymore? Cool."

She shook her head. "If you knew who he was in his entirety, you'd understand why you being alive after leaving a body in front of his club is a fine act of mercy."

"I heard."

"He offered you his intimacy. He doesn't do that often, you know?"

"He didn't fuck me. You did."

"He allowed you to be in his presence during an intimate moment. It's coming. Is that what you want?"

I hesitated to answer, not trying to come off as thirsty. "I mean, yeah, I guess."

"It's okay, you can tell me." She winked.

"I want it."

She nodded. "It's coming. He's becoming very fond of you. Personally, I don't see why. Don't take it the wrong way, but it's just that I know his type. You're beautiful, don't get me wrong, but he's into a more mature woman."

"Like you, huh?"

"I'm not the only woman he has."

I swallowed the lump in my throat. "What?"

"Oh, no. How do you think he's been on the streets so long?"

"Clearly, he's a sociopath."

"He's attracted to women of power: judges, lawyers, doctors, detectives, and so on. He breaks down the strongest woman, and then he builds her back up to an even stronger woman. We appreciate that. Don't we?"

I nodded. "You know what's wild? Just three days in his basement and it changed me. I'm moving differently." I pointed at Fray. "This man should've been dead, but this approach was far more effective. I appreciate that. I'm just scared."

"You're scared of how much three days changed you because you feel yourself being broken down, too. Even without the sex."

"I see you went through this stage of confusion."

"Indeed. But the total outcome was beautiful. I'm extremely blessed to have met him."

"When did you meet him?"

"He found me years ago. His son had been shot and rushed into the hospital. He flew in all the way from Jamaica to be at his son's side. I couldn't keep my eyes off him. He was like a magnet."

"He has a son? Really? Where?"

She looked as if she'd said too much. "Those are intimate details about his life that you should ask him and not me."

"Got it. So, what made you fall in love? Are you in love?"

"Very much so. He's my husband."

"What?"

I could tell she was used to the shock. "Yes. We're married. We have an open marriage but to a certain extent."

"And what's that?" I asked, still appalled by her answer. I thought she would just be a friend. The two seemed very detached but attached at the same time.

"I wanted a traditional marriage because I'm a traditional woman, but I know the man I married. I wouldn't dare change him. My only request is that he loves me and only me and that he doesn't have any children outside of the children we already have and the ones we may have in the future."

"Do you get along with his older kids?"

"I do."

"What about him? Does he?"

"He has a tough way of showing love, but he loves his kids very much. They know and understand."

"It's wild to know that he's been in the city this long, and I've never heard of him."

"He's the best kept secret. You've probably seen his work and didn't know. I'm almost one hundred percent sure you know at least one of his older sons. If he allows questions about his life, you should ask him one day. Everyone in his life is dedicated and loyal to him, no matter how hard his love is. He's reliable. He's always there. But when a bridge is burnt, he has that same switch that he taught me to have."

"He can turn cold?"

Her eyes lowered. "Cold isn't the word. Whatever you do, never lie to him. Never disrespect him. Now that you know better, he won't be so nice next time."

"What happens if I do?"

"Don't."

"I'll try not to." She didn't respond, just continued with the surgery. "Does your family like him?"

"They adore him. Like I said, he's a man's man. He's always there for them. Delyle is the go-to man for anyone who knows him."

"That must be so tiring."

"He can't function without being Superman. I understand it. Trust me, I've tried to get through to him, but I can't. He loves being the man anyone can depend on."

"I'm excited to see where this goes. You don't ever worry about him falling in love with someone else?"

"Nope, I don't. He has this ability to have a deep sexual

attraction to someone without loving them. That person may fall in love, but he knows how to not love someone without hurting them. It's called respect and loyalty. Hopefully, you'll get to experience him. I want that for you." She sounded genuine.

I mean, she was there doing something that could possibly land her in prison, so I had reason to trust what she said.

"I'm scared I might piss him off and get myself killed like I almost did when he and I first met."

"Just be honest. That's all he really asks of anyone." She finished up and placed clean bandages around the scarred area. "Hold open that Ziploc bag for me. Make sure nothing touches outside gloves," she said as she held Fray's manhood in the palm of her hands like sand.

"Will he be sore?"

"Yes. I left some meds to keep him from feeling pain until he heals." She dumped the rest of him into the bag and placed it into a bucket.

"Why are we leaving him meds? He needs to suffer."

"Him not having a penis anymore is suffering enough. We don't want to be greedy. We don't want him in physical pain when he doesn't have to be. That's when rage gets involved. You're right, we didn't have to leave the meds for pain, but we did." She cleaned the area and put the bloody plastic into the medium-sized bucket also. Then, she drained the blood into the sink and washed it down with a gallon of bleach that she had in her roller suitcase.

She handed me a scrub with some homemade spray that smelled like bleach and something else. "Try not to miss a spot."

We scrubbed until it was squeaky clean on and around the table where the surgery was performed.

"Step back and turn all the lights off."

"Okay." I did as I was told, and she turned on a black light. There was one small line of blood that showed up, and it was around the sink. She wiped it, and it disappeared.

"I'm impressed," she said.

"You've cleaned crime scenes before. Haven't you?"

"To put myself through school, I cleaned crime scenes. I know my way around blood."

"This crime shit comes with a lot."

"You have no idea," she said. "And there you were, thinking that killing was the only answer."

I motioned toward Fray. "Do we wait for him to wake up?"

Veronica pulled another syringe from the pocket of her large roller suitcase. She thumped it and pressed just a squirt out. "No. I'm about to fill his veins with adrenaline. Step back. He's going to be intensely confused the first few moments."

I did as I was told and stepped back. She stabbed his chest with the syringe and pressed down to release the fluid. She stepped back just a little and watched him while watching the time on his clock.

"Did it work?"

She tapped her foot impatiently. "Three, two, one." And just like that, he jerked up like he had just almost drowned and tried to catch his breath. He grabbed his chest.

I laughed because that was the least of his worries.

His eyes immediately found me. "What have you done? What happened to me? What the fuck is that smell?" He tried to get up to move, but Veronica rushed over to help him. He tried to swing, which she expected, so she moved slightly to the left.

"That smell is only in your head. It smells like rubber, but it's not. It's the adrenaline pumping through your heart. You haven't noticed yet, but your penis and ball sacks are completely gone."

Fray almost laughed but was still panicked. He touched the bandages under the fresh towel, and it all made sense to him. I was expecting more rage, but what I got was tears. He sobbed. His lips even poked out like a child. I didn't care. I couldn't care. I got the same pleasure that he got from watching me scream all those times he raped me. Now, it was all coming together.

This was so much better than killing him. I actually got to

watch him die on the inside, and it felt like soaking in the sun at the beach.

"We've left you medications strong enough to help with the pain until you have completely healed. I don't think I have to remind you that these pain pills are strong and should not be taken at once."

"Why? Why do this to me?" he asked, looking directly at me. "I've kept you out of jail. I've cared for you and given you what you wanted. Why?"

I saw Veronica cringe. "We just helped you fight a demon," I said.

"It was taking you out, so we took it out of you. No need to thank us. It was free of charge. We have the video of Arielle being molested, so think twice before you try and go to the police."

"How will I urinate?" he asked.

She pointed to the bag attached to his stomach. "The bag is reusable. Once it fills, untwist it, pour it out, and twist the cap back. Those are the good ones. You'll be fine."

After explaining a little more to him, she and I both left. Outside, we said our goodbyes and went our separate ways. Since I knew Veronica wasn't home, I felt comfortable calling Delyle, but only when I got close to my loft.

He answered with a groggy voice. "Did you ping me to any towers close to his home?"

"No," I answered quickly. "I waited until I got home."

"Good. How did it go?"

"It actually went well. Your wife is a very sweet woman."

"I see she likes you."

"Why you say that?"

"She opened up enough to tell you we're married."

"She also told me you guys have children and how she met you at her job. She said you had sons my age but left the rest for you to tell me."

"Okay. So, she *really* likes you."

"That's a good thing?"

"That's a great thing."

"How so?"

"Because next time we meet, she won't have to be there. I'll call you with the details later. How do you feel?"

"I actually feel amazing and liberated. Life just looks so different from where I'm standing right now. You know?"

"I know. I'm happy for you. You can now focus on becoming a better you without a coward invading your space."

"Thanks for that."

"It's no problem. Get some rest."

"Okay."

"Night."

"Night," I said and hung up, knowing I didn't want to.

SPIN
SOMETHING STRANGE

It was well past midnight when there was a knock at the door. Diamond would usually bark, but she ran away a few days ago, so Terry and I weren't afforded that luxury.

Terry grabbed his gun and headed to the front door with me not too far behind. He got to the door before me, so I could read his body language and tell there wasn't a threat at the door, but there was definitely an inconvenience. He placed the gun on the sofa. While he bent down, I saw a woman standing there in a nursing fit. She had bone straight hair with brown, smooth skin. Her brows were perfectly shaded, and her baby hairs were laid. She had real baby hairs, not the forced ones. This woman was beautiful. Looked to have some Indian somewhere in her bloodline.

"What's going on?" I asked, moving closer to the door. That's when I saw Diamond sitting behind the girl.

"This is my ex-girlfriend, Crystal. Diamond ran to her house, and she was just bringing her back," Terry said as he walked around Crystal and snatched Diamond by the collar. "Get yo' ass in this house."

Diamond cried out in pain as he pinched her ear. She ran past me and laid low in her cage.

"She couldn't just wait until normal hours to bring her back?" I asked, tightening my robe.

Terry looked at me like, *don't do this shit right now.*

"I work overnight, and I will be busy most of the day when I'm not sleeping, so I decided to bring her on my lunch break."

Terry intervened. Standing in the middle of us, he said, "Thanks, Crystal. I owe you one." He tried to close the door, but she placed her palm on the door.

"Icis is gone again," she said.

"Who's Icis?" I wanted to know.

"It's his mother." The disgusted look on her face made me want to slap her. It's like she was mad that I didn't know his mama's name. He didn't like talking about his mother or father. What was I supposed to do? Beat it out of him?

"I was talking to *my* man."

She smirked and shook her head. She was hurt to see me there. The break-up must have been more recent than I thought. "*Your* man, huh?" She glanced over at Terry, who looked tired and annoyed.

"Crystal, I'll handle it. Thanks for bringing Diamond."

"You'll handle what?!"

"Spin, go the FUCK to bed before you piss me off. She brought me my damn dog. What's the problem? You act like I'm fucking the bitch."

"Bitch?" She folded her arms and looked at him as if she'd never heard him say that to her before. I noticed she never raised her voice. She handled my man with too much care, and I didn't like that. She was very gentle with him.

"You know I ain't mean it like that."

"Yes, the fuck you did!" I screamed at him.

She backed away and took a good look at us. "Is that my robe?"

I looked down at the robe I was wearing. "No, it's *my* mama's robe."

"It's mine. He was so in a rush when he left me for you that he took some of my things."

"This robe belongs to this bitch?"

"What's up with the disrespect? Have I disrespected either of you?" she asked.

I stepped outside the threshold and toward her. "You can have this robe back, bitch, and you can get hit while you're here. Who the fuck do you think you are?" I asked as Terry pulled me back and placed me behind him.

"Thank you, Crystal. Goodnight, and sorry for the confusion."

"What the fuck are you apologizing for? Huh? You care about this bitch still or what? Because I can leave right now and leave you and her to it."

Terry didn't say anything, just looked at me like he wanted to choke me. He then took his attention off me and put it back on Crystal. "Thanks again. Good night."

She nodded and walked toward the stairs. "Does she know?" she asked with her hand on the railing, turning to face us.

"Know what?" I wanted to know.

"Nothing."

"She doesn't know. Does she? That's why you left me? Is that why you love her so much? Or do you even love her? Maybe it's pity."

"What the fuck is she talking about?"

Crystal turned and walked away, saying nothing else. He slammed the door shut and locked Diamond in her cage. He then stormed to the bedroom, and I stormed right behind him.

"What was that secret code shit you and her had going on?"

"Go to sleep, Spin."

I snatched the covers from him. It shocked me how quickly he was on both feet. He towered over me with his fist balled like he wanted to smack my head against the TV.

Being careful to choose my words wisely, I said, "I just want to know what's going on."

"She brought my dog back. What else you want to know?"

"What was she talking about when she said I must not know? What don't I know?"

"I don't know what she's talking about. Let's go to bed now."

I stood my ground. "No."

Having lost patience with me, he took a deep breath and snatched my robe off, leaving me ass naked. With all his strength, he grabbed me by the neck and pushed me down onto the bed.

"Terry, stop. We need to talk about this."

"Not doing this shit with you tonight." He pulled his dick from his briefs, spit in his palm, and massaged it around the head of his manhood. He then slid it deep inside me, catching me off guard. I gasped for air from having my breath taken away.

"Terry," I moaned.

"Shut up. We about to go to sleep." He stroked me hard with my head pinned down. The harder I fought, the tighter he held me down and fucked me. My ass bounced against his pelvis. His hands traveled from my neck to my waist as he allowed me to join him instead of fighting him. I threw my ass back and began to welcome him inside of me.

"Why you fucking me like this? Shit."

He yanked me by my hair and continued dicking me down until I undeniably climaxed. He didn't cum; instead, he removed his dick from me and stood back.

"Get under the covers."

"But, Terry—"

"I said get under the covers." He meant everything he said tonight. He wanted to go to sleep and for me to stop bothering him with questions about Crystal. I was afraid to proceed, knowing this was a warning instead of a late sex session.

I did as I was told and tucked myself into bed. He did the same and turned his back to me. Instantly, he dozed off to sleep. As for me? I pulled out my phone and followed a hunch I had from earlier when Crystal showed up.

The other day, I received a friend request from a Crystal

McFrank, but it disappeared. If I wasn't mistaken, I saw her at the grocery store too. I wasn't sure until I went to her Facebook page and saw her face. It was her—the girl from the grocery store. I knew I wasn't tripping, so I sent a friend request back.

Crystal was beautiful in pictures and in person. I didn't understand what made him want to leave someone like her. From what I saw on her page, she was very successful and well put together. She was a nurse supervisor at Medical City on the overnight shift. Her brother had also just passed, and she seemed to be taking it well. I loved her sweet tone and nonaggression. She even smelled good, like brown sugar.

Scrolling through her Facebook, I saw nothing but condolences for a while and then some old pictures of her and her deceased brother. As I scrolled deeper and deeper, I saw nothing but pictures of her and Terry from a while back. Those pictures went on for years and years. I saw him and her grow younger and younger the further I went down. He seemed to have loved her very much, so I couldn't understand what would make him want to leave her for me.

A notification popped up, telling me that she'd accepted my request. Before going to sleep, I waited and waited to see if she would message me and hop on some dumb shit, but she didn't. So, I went to sleep with my man holding me.

Sway
Family Over Everything

As I brushed my teeth, I listened to Mama Crystal grill me about spending time with Arielle. She said that ever since I came to get her three days ago, all she'd been talking about was how she wished we'd spend more time together. I loved my little sister, but sometimes I felt like Mama Crystal put too much of a burden on me to spend time with Arielle. She never cursed Asha or Tweety into coming to pick her up, only me. I had things to do. I even felt bad about having her with me to handle the business with Fray.

Speaking of Fray, I hadn't heard from him on calls or in person ever since he was emasculated. I would be lying if I said that I wasn't worried about an initial response, but he didn't give me a hard time. He had emailed me, thanking me for my urine sample that I didn't give him, and that was it. I was starting to feel like maybe I should listen to Delyle more often. He knew something about what he spoke about.

It still tripped me out how it all panned out with him and me.

After getting myself together, Spin brought breakfast that she'd just cooked into my room. "Just a cheese omelet." She handed me the paper plate.

I sat down briefly to eat it. I had things to do today and wanted to get Arielle out of the way.

"Rel seems to still be feeling some type of way about Laytron," Spin said.

"Why you say that?"

"She called off last night at the trap. Once again, Tweety had to fill in for her, and you know how she felt about it."

"I'm starting to feel like maybe Rel should be replaced or just completely removed."

"I think we all are starting to feel that way," she agreed.

"You think she's told anyone about Laytron?"

"No. Asha would've known." I took a bite from the large, cheese-filled goodness.

"I'm just thinking about the night we drilled him. Before we knew it was Asha, Rel was talking. I can't get over that." For Spin to bring this up, it had to be something wrong. She usually would let people slide with things.

"Yeah, I was thinking about that, too. Let's just watch her moves first and see what happens."

"Cool." She turned her head, and that's when I saw a passion mark on her neck. I playfully nudged her shoulder. "What?"

"You been getting busy. I realized you ain't been here."

She tried to cover it. "It's nothing."

"Looks like you've been having a great time."

"You heard about that cop that was killed?" she asked, changing the subject.

"Hell yeah. Everyone heard about it. Why?"

She bit her nails with her elbow resting on her wrist. "Just asking. That was crazy."

"It was." For some reason, seeing Asha and Demaris at the same time crossed my mind. "Hey, what do you think about Demaris?"

She looked at me as if the question was random and odd. "I think what everyone thinks: he's a menace and a psychopath. I wouldn't be surprised if he's the one who killed that officer." She said that jokingly, but I thought he did.

Being in the streets like we were, it was quickly learned that nothing was a coincidence. Knowing that one thing could be the difference between life and death. That being said, the shooting occurred right by Asha's place, right around the time she and Demaris disappeared. I was sure she knew.

After eating, I left to pick up Arielle. Usually, I would call to let her know I was outside, but she was sitting on the porch with her purse, waiting for me.

I always felt like Arielle's birth mother was a whore who got pregnant by an Italian man. Arielle had the most beautiful green eyes and long lashes. Her brows looked naturally arched, and her lips were plump like Puerto Ricans. Her hair was curly and long, down to the middle of her back. For a fourteen-year-old, she had a body like a grown woman. That's why we were so overprotective of her. Of course, she wasn't a virgin, but none of us were by the time we were that age, not in our hood.

Arielle was different from us, though. She was so sweet, even when she hit puberty. We never had to deal with the stank attitude like most siblings and parents had to, and for that, we were all thankful. Having her in our lives was like a breath of fresh air. She did what she was told, kept the house clean, and her grades never dropped below a B plus.

Today, she had her hair down and parted in the middle. Her natural curls were popping. She wore a sundress with some nude sandals I'd bought her. She had this on three days ago. I had an uneasy feeling in the pit of my stomach.

She saw me, and her face beamed with joy. "Mama, I'm gone!" she yelled inside the house and locked the door.

Once in the car, she kissed me on the cheek and immediately got to talking. "I'm so happy to see you. Mama has been working my nerves."

"She's been home?"

"No, not really. But when she is home, she's getting on my last nerve."

"Why are you wearing the same clothes from three days ago? Me, Asha, and Tweety give Mom a few hundred every week for bills and for you."

She frowned and slowly leaned back against the seat. "That's what I wanted to talk to you about."

I didn't push the issue. I knew once we were settled and where we needed to be, she would open up to me.

We ended up at Joe Pool Lake, sitting on the benches and eating ice cream. It was a beautiful, scorching hot day. Good thing we had the wind blowing, or I wouldn't have been able to take it.

"So, what's wrong?"

"I didn't want to say anything, but Ma is on drugs again."

"Okay, she's been on drugs."

She looked at me and placed her hand on mine. "No, Sway, she's on *drugs drugs* again. It's getting bad again."

"Like using all her money on it bad? Selling your belongings for it bad?"

"Yes. She also has this new man that she gives money to all the time because he also does drugs."

I tossed my ice cream cone into the water and shook my head. My appetite was gone. "She promised."

"I know she did, but she broke that promise. Sway, I have to hide things from her, but she will tear my room up until she finds them. That's why I never go anywhere no more. I have to watch my things."

"How have you been getting money?" I gave her a deep, concerned look. "And don't lie to me. It's nothing you can tell me that the rest of us didn't go through with Mama."

"My old English teacher gives me money, but I don't like asking him."

Oh, God. "Him?"

"Yes. He's married."

"And what does he make you do for the money?"

"He makes me spend time with him when his wife is at church. He has a massage table, and he makes me receive massages."

"Is he fucking you during these massages?"

"No."

I sighed. "Thank God."

"He fucks me *after* the massages."

A tear dropped from my eye. Arielle was truly my weakness. Hell, my family was my weakness. We'd all been through so much, way before we even hit ten years old. We'd all seen things that no kids should've seen.

"Why didn't you tell us, Arielle? We give Mom all this money, and it's plenty where it came from. You know all you have to do is ask, and whatever you want is yours."

"She didn't want you all to know I didn't have money because y'all would know she was on drugs bad again."

As she silently cried, I pulled out some money I had in my purse. Grabbing her hand, I closed the money tight in her palm. "It's a little over four thousand. Put the money in your tampon boxes but leave them out in the bathroom cabinet with tampons at the top. For some reason, she never went through our tampon boxes." I knew why she never touched any tampon boxes. When I first started my period, Houston had to steal tampons for me. If I didn't have them, none of us had them, and we would bleed everywhere. Mama Crystal hated doing laundry. "If you hide the box, she'll get suspicious."

"Okay. Thank you, Sway." She put the money in her purse.

"Get you some new clothes."

"Where will I hide them?"

"You won't have to. Even if I have to whoop her ass every day for touching your things, she won't. I promise."

"Okay." She laid her head on my shoulder. "Mama said she was going to get herself together, and I believed her."

"We always do. She did almost a decade keeping it under control. I wonder what triggered her."

"She keeps trying to teach me survival skills. Saying I need to learn to fend for myself because she won't always be here."

"You think she's sick?"

"I know she is."

I then looked back on the last few times I'd seen her. She was losing more and more weight. Mama Crystal's weight always fluctuated. That's why I thought nothing of it.

"What will happen to me if something happens to Ma? I don't want to go to a group home. I'm scared."

"The courts won't give you to me and Tweety because we have records, but they will give you to Asha. But that will cause so much shit."

"Like what?"

"An investigation on us."

"I don't understand."

"Asha didn't mention to the police department that she was siblings to any of the Spindarellas. Nobody really knows unless they knew us as kids. But even as kids, Asha never really hung around us. She was different." I pinched her nose. "Just like you."

She giggled. "Really? Asha was different?" Arielle's beautiful eyes lit up.

She loved hearing how we were as kids. She was only a baby when she got with us. Mama Crystal was trusted by CPS. Everyone knew she was the sweetest. An old church member used to work with CPS before she passed and would allow Mama Crystal to get foster kids, so she could get money and eventually adopt them. She loved us all like we were her own. She had real kids, too, before us. They all were raised by their dads.

"Yeah, Asha was always sneaking away to the courthouse to get visitor passes so she could watch trials. She's always wanted to be a detective."

"Isn't her real mother dead?"

"Yes."

"They never found who did it? Right?"

"Yeah. On her seventh birthday. It took them years and years to figure out what Asha already knew."

"Who did it?"

"Asha's uncle. It was her real dad's brother. Long story," I said, taking a deep breath. I didn't feel like talking about our lives. I cringed when I thought about it.

"I want to sing, Sway." One thing about Arielle is she didn't talk for years. We thought she was autistic. Her first words were songs. Her voice was soft and beautiful like Aaliyah's.

"You should get serious about it. Every time we try to get serious about it, you freeze up."

"I don't know what I'm afraid of."

"Your own damn potential," I joked with her.

"Maybe so."

"You got a man? Have you been taking your birth control? You using condoms?"

"No. Yes. Yes. I don't have a man. I've been taking my birth control, and I do indeed use condoms."

"Who you been fucking?"

"It's this guy. He's a little older."

"How much older, Arielle? Please don't start that shit."

"He's nineteen."

"Okay, that's not bad."

"He plays college basketball and is on the draft list."

"What round?"

"First."

"Impressive."

"He's in love. He wants me to come with him to Miami. He's getting drafted to the Miami Heat."

"How he know?"

"They've already been training him."

"You want to go?"

She shook her head. "Nah."

"Why not?"

"I'm still a kid. I don't want to drop out."

"Go to school in Miami. Or take the test to graduate early. You're damn sure smart enough."

"You right."

"Whatever you do, just please don't get pregnant yet." I held my pinky out to her.

"I won't. Pinky promise."

We talked for hours before we finally left. I bought her some groceries so she could cook for the rest of the week. "Make sure you cook food for the week, so she can't sell the food before it's cooked. She can't sell it if it's already cooked," I said as I helped her with the bags.

Once in the house, I told her to go to her room after we put the groceries up. I was about to talk to Mama Crystal or threaten her, and I didn't want Arielle to hear.

She was on the phone, in bed, watching her stories. I instantly started to rampage through her drawers. That's where she kept everything. She hung up the phone and ran over, trying to stop me. I yanked my hand back and gave her a death stare. She backed away and started pulling at her hair. She knew it was over.

"Where is it?" I started tossing clothes everywhere. "Where the fuck is it?!"

"Okay!" She pointed at the bottom drawer.

"The sock drawer? You're getting clever." I pulled out the bags and held them in my hand. I didn't see a lot of needles. "Again? You back on heroin? Not just powder? Heroin? Fucking heroin, Ma?!"

"I know. Just listen." She watched the drugs in my hand like a hawk. She wanted to make sure I didn't throw them away.

"Fuck that. You've been stealing from Arielle for this shit? She's not going through what the fuck we went through! Do you understand me?"

She didn't answer, and I didn't have the patience. I took the drugs to the toilet, opened them, and started pouring them in.

"No!" She reached for the bags, but I kicked her in the stomach, sending her flying into the bathtub.

When I got down to the very last bag, she dropped to her knees and burst into tears. "I'm dying!"

My heart dropped because I had that feeling while at the lake. It was all starting to make sense. "What?"

"I have AIDS. Went to the doctor a few weeks ago for a cough that wouldn't go away, and that's what it was."

"How? They have so many meds for that shit. Nobody is dying from that no more."

"Nobody is dying from HIV anymore, but I have full blown AIDS, Sway. It sat for too long."

"Those needles? You always want to be so nice to your junkie friends and share your needles. I know that's what it is. I give you money. We give you money! You couldn't get clean needles!" This day was emotionally destroying to me. I was built for this, but I couldn't handle it right now. "Instead of getting help, you kill yourself faster? What about Arielle? Do you even care about her?"

"She doesn't need me. She'll be better off. Look what I'm doing to her. Look what I did to y'all."

"You loved us. You raised us. You cared for us."

"Y'all some fucking murderers and gang bangers. I ruined y'all. I heard Tweety and Arielle talking when she bought her home three days ago. I know what she did. She helped you set a man up and emasculate him and ain't batted a lash. She's been sleeping peacefully at night, knowing what she's done."

"You don't know what he did to me. What he's been doing to me."

"I know, and I understand, but that little girl in there was ruined way before this. It's all because of me. Them people gave me these kids, and I should've given y'all back. You and your sisters had to suck dick and steal to take care of me when y'all was just kids. I should've been taking care of y'all, not the other way around. And now I've ruined my baby, too."

We both stood there breathing hard. Arielle had come into the room and was now crying by the TV. I looked at the last bag in my hand and threw it at Mama Crystal. She caught it and went back to crying. I couldn't do this today.

"Arielle, remember what I said. I'll call and check on y'all later." I rushed out of the house, pulling my dreads away from my face.

As I drove off, I called Delyle. He hadn't called back when he said he would, and I just needed his advice. His advice hadn't failed me yet. "I was just about to call you," he answered.

"I'm sorry to bother you. I was wondering if I could stop by. Maybe get some of your expertise."

"Sure. I'm at the club. We aren't open yet, but you can definitely come while they set up."

"Thanks."

"No problem."

I stopped and got some crackers from the gas station. That's about all I could put on my stomach without completely regurgitating it back up.

When I got to the club, he had me park in the back by the dumpster. He locked the door behind me and took me up the elevator to the loft.

"You look nice." I sat at the small bar and watched him finish using his machine to count money. He had on some slacks with a V-neck and some loafers. As always, he smelled so good.

"How old are you?" I wanted to know.

"Forty-five."

"I wasn't too far off. You don't look bad for your age. You look gorgeous."

"So do you. You've been crying."

"I have."

"Would you like to talk about it?"

"Not really."

He nodded and smiled, still putting more money into the machine and putting rubber bands on it once the stacks got too thick. "So, we have to do the cat and mouse thing first."

"It's my mom. I just found out she's back on drugs again, and she's selling my little sister's clothes."

"That's not the part that's bothering you the most. Is it?"

I shook my head. "Can I have a shot?"

"Sure." He waited until the last money in one pile was counted and slid a D'usse bottle over to me with a shot glass. He then went back to counting his money.

"She has AIDS."

"Lucky for you guys, it isn't a death sentence like it used to be."

"Yeah, but she won't get help. She decided to do more drugs and kill herself faster."

"Why is she deciding anything?"

I was left speechless. He had a point. "She's your mom, but this ain't the time to look at her like a mother. Look at her like you would a regular junkie who you cared about. What would you do?"

"I would do what I did with the last one. Give her one chance for rehab, and that's it. I would tell her if she blows it, I will kill her. Not only will I kill her, but I will torture her. That's my mom, so I would never torture her."

"But you *would* kill her?"

"Correct."

"She needs to know that."

"How?"

"You're still looking at her like a mother, and you can't do that. Your little sister's life is on the line. If your mother dies, where will she go?"

"I don't know. Maybe with Asha. Tweety drinks too much. But even with that being said, I can't have that happen."

"Because then the courts will find out that Asha is related to the Spindarellas."

I love how I didn't have to overexplain anything to him. He just understood. "Exactly."

"With all of this on the line, why would you even consider letting her decide anything for herself?"

"I wasn't thinking about that."

"It should be the only thing you think of when you think of her. She's about to risk it all, being careless. Handle it."

The shots had started to take the edge off. "Is your mother still around."

"Yes."

"Here?"

"No."

Okay, so he didn't want to get that deep into his life. "How many children do you have?"

"Nine."

"Oh, wow. How old are they?"

"I had my first when I was fifteen. Do the math."

"So, your oldest is thirty?"

"Correct." He was excellent at multitasking. He was now counting the money by hand after it left the machine. He didn't trust anything.

"What happened to you and your first child's mother?"

"I have six children with the first and three with Veronica."

"Impressive."

"What's so impressive about it?"

"Do you take care of all of them?"

"Yes. My oldest six are grown enough to take care of themselves, but I'm still there to pick up where they lack. My youngest three are well taken care of, too."

"Did your kids ever stress you out while growing up?"

He laughed and started a new stack of money. Money was all over the kitchen and the bar. I had never seen this much money in my life, and I was sure it was just his play money. "They definitely stressed me out. Not all of them. My youngest two, with my first love, stressed me out. They still do. One is always having girlfriend problems. The other one is a lot like you."

"What am I like?"

"Hard headed. Trigger happy. Moves like he has nothing to lose once he's mad enough."

"How many grandkids do you have?"

"My oldest three have four kids each. That's not counting the other ones. So, if three kids have me with twelve, use your imagination."

"Almost twenty?"

"Maybe." He winked at me and went back to counting.

"You take care of your grandkids too?"

"For the most part, my kids are very self-sufficient. My grandkids love me dearly, and I love them. I'll do anything for them."

"All of them live in Texas?"

He shook his head. "Nope. They're scattered, but that's fine. I travel." I crossed my arms and zeroed in on his eyes. He caught me. "What's up?"

"What made you the way you are?"

"How am I?" He asked me like I'd just asked him.

"Different."

"I don't know. Life."

"Have you ever been afraid of anything?"

"Yes."

"When?"

"I'll just tell you about the day you already know about; the day my son was shot. I didn't think he would make it. Nobody thought he would make it. I'm scared for him every day. Every time I talk to him, I feel like it will be my last. He's reckless. But I love him to death."

"The way you are with women, are you like that with your family?"

"That's sick."

"Not like that. I mean, detached. Could you hold them in a basement when they piss you off?"

"Oh, okay. No, I never put any of my children in a basement. They are my offspring."

"You put me in a basement."

"You also left a dead body in front of my establishment. Not to mention, you aren't my offspring."

"True. So, what made you fall for Veronica?"

"You talked to her. I'm sure you liked her, too. Her personality and she knows how to compartmentalize." I looked up, trying to see if I knew what that word meant. "It means she knows how to separate things. She knows when to be my wife, and she knows when to be my fantasy."

"Do you guys have code words?"

"No. She just knows me." He stacked another pile of money and went to the next. "She wouldn't give up. She was determined to be in my life just as bad as I was determined to be in hers. We just ended up like this. Neither of us knows how we fell in love. We just did. I woke up one day, and she had a conference to go to. That's when I realized I didn't want to be without her."

"That's romantic."

"Is it?"

"Yes, for you."

"You said that like you know me."

"I don't know you. Not even sure if you would let me know you."

"It's different parts to me that you can know. Some parts, you will never know, and you will be fine with that. Trust me. Enough of me, let's talk about you."

"What about me? Ask me anything."

"How do you feel after you've killed someone, love?"

That question caught me completely off guard. "I feel like... I feel... I feel nothing."

"Why do you feel nothing?"

"I don't know. I just don't feel anything."

"Before you went with your foster mother, what happened?"

I swallowed the lump in my throat. "A lot." Thinking back gave me chills.

"You don't have to answer anything you don't want to answer."

"I don't remember much. I only remember the things I can't forget."

"Deep. Like what?"

"My grandmother burning me with cigarettes." Just talking about it gave me feelings. I could feel the sting and smell of my skin burning.

"Is that what those marks are on your wrist?"

"Yes."

"Why would she burn you?"

"I don't know. I never knew why. I just remember trying not to breathe around her. It seemed like whenever she saw me, it was a problem. So, I tried to stay out of her way."

"What made the system finally take you from her?"

"My uncle came home from the military for the first time since I had been born. I was seven. He never came around. His dad raised him. My mama stayed with my grandma until the day she died. My uncle only came because he heard rumors from family and old friends that my grandma was abusing me. When he saw that it was true, he took me from her and got her arrested."

"Do you hear from your uncle?"

"I used to. He hates who I've become, so he keeps his distance."

"Are you happy he took you?"

"Yes, I am very thankful. I was just hurt because he couldn't take me. He said the life he lived wasn't for a little girl. He cried and cried when he dropped me off. But he dropped me off."

"Where is he now."

"I don't know."

"Would you like to find him?"

"No."

"What about your grandma?"

"I don't know. She's been out of prison for over ten years."

"You have no interest in making amends with her?"

"None whatsoever. I don't need her."

"When was the last time you were scared?"

"Today. Hearing Ma tell me she was dying, I hadn't felt fear like that in years."

"Are you afraid of her dying or what it means if she dies?"

"Both."

"Why are you here?" he flat out asked.

"Huh?"

"You keep finding your way to wherever I am. Why?"

"Is it a problem?"

"No, it's not a problem at all. I just want to get a feel of you."

I shrugged. "I never had a father figure or any guidance at all, and I get that with you. I like what's happened to me since the day we met."

"That's nice to hear. Happy I had that effect on you."

"Why do you let me come around?"

He grinned like he knew that was coming next. "I like your willingness to be taught."

"That's new to me. I didn't know I could be this way."

"What I've found out in life is that at your age, you really aren't who you think you are. At that age, I wasn't who I thought I was either."

"That's the part that scares me."

"It should. The mind is very tricky."

"It is. How did you handle not being who you thought you were?"

"I handled it pretty well, I must say," he told me.

"What pleases you sexually?" I finally asked. I saw the dungeon. I saw the toys. Now I wanted to know what brought out the beast.

"I'm the dominant one. What about you?"

"So am I. I like for my partner to do exactly as I say to please me. I've never found it appealing being the submissive."

"Why don't you like being submissive?"

"I don't know why."

"Would you like to find out why?"

"I'm afraid to find out why, if we're being honest."

"You're afraid of what you may find. You're afraid that you are indeed not who you thought you were."

"Yes."

"It's fine. I understand." He was finally done counting money. Now I had his full attention. "Come." He held out his hand for mine. He then led me to the living room area. "Get on your knees."

"Why?"

"Ask me why again, and you're leaving. I don't like repeating myself."

I did as I was told and got down on my knees. Of course, I was anxious about what would happen next but also nervous. Delyle was unpredictable, to say the least. I never knew what to expect. Us being in this predicament was one of the reasons he confused me. I kept asking myself how I got into this situation.

He walked near me, his dick print staring me in the face. "Can I touch it?" I asked.

"Yes, you may."

I slowly reached my hand out and felt his dick. It was rock hard. I traced the long beast to the middle of his thigh and found a curve. My clit jumped. It was wide and long. I'd never experienced one quite like this. Medium-sized dicks were more of my thing because I couldn't handle big ones. I didn't know if I couldn't, or maybe I didn't want to. All I knew was that I ached to feel him inside me.

"Open your mouth." I did as I was told and awaited further instructions. This felt surprisingly good. Knowing that he wanted to command me is what did it for me. He pulled his member out and teased the tip with my bottom lip. "Kiss it."

I kissed it.

"Slower."

So, I French kissed his dick.

"Now, open wide." He said as he pushed himself more into my mouth. Just as I was about to close my lips and suck, his cellular rang. "Once second, don't move."

"Okay."

He walked away to answer his phone, looking down at the club from the window. "Coming down now." He hung up the phone. "I'll be right back. Do not move a muscle. Stay exactly how you are. Understand?"

"Yes."

He grinned and left me alone. As I sat on my knees, I couldn't help but smile. I wanted more of him. He gave me so little that the bits and pieces he did give, I was thankful for. I could only imagine how it felt to get all of him like Veronica had.

I got anxious to know who was down there, so I quickly got up to look and immediately wished I hadn't. What I saw, I didn't know how to feel about it.

When I saw him coming back towards the elevator, I got right back into my position. He slowly walked over to me and stared down into my eyes. "Did you move?"

I wanted to lie, but I remembered what his wife said. She said never lie to him no matter what. "Yes, I did."

"Thanks for your honesty. It goes a long way."

"Who was the guy you handed a package to?"

"He's my son."

"That's surprising." I sat on my knees, wondering what was next. He didn't say anything else or even make a facial expression.

"Leave."

"Leave?"

"You disobeyed a simple order. Leave, and if I do decide to see you again, I will call you. Do not call me."

I stood as he grabbed my purse and handed it to me. "Delyle, please."

"Don't make me say it again."

I wanted to plead with him, but his mind was already made. I knew when someone's mind was made, it was no changing it. Especially a man of his caliber.

"I'm sorry, Delyle." I let my head fall down as he walked me to the elevator. He then walked me out the back door, waited until I drove away, and closed the door back.

At least he was always a gentleman, no matter what he felt. Respect was instilled in him at a very young age. It was very obvious.

I left his club full of regret. I wondered what would've happened if I hadn't moved. Would he be fucking me senseless right now? Would I ever get the opportunity again?

Most importantly, how didn't I know that Terry was his son?

ASHA
FAMILY VIOLENCE

I couldn't even enjoy my lunch break with Demaris because Arielle kept blowing my phone up. It was nothing but her and Mama Crystal getting into it again. I didn't have the patience to deal with Mama Crystal and bullshit. Not today. I was cramping on my period and had a headache that made my head feel heavy as a bowling ball.

I had an hour lunch and used it to go home and cuddle up under Demaris while he rubbed my stomach. "Answer. It might be important."

"No. It's damn near four in the morning. She better have that damn basketball player pick her up. She knows how to get the fuck from around Mama Crystal if she wants to. I'm not doing this today."

"If she calls again, you're answering. I ain't trying to hear nothing you talking about. That girl is fourteen and being raised by a junkie. Don't do her like that."

"We all were raised by her. She'll be okay."

Just as he laid his head on my stomach, my radio went off. "Officer Wynn?"

I hurriedly reached on my belt buckle and pressed the *Talk* button. "Go ahead."

"This is Gary at the station. Please call my personal line."

"Copy that."

"Here." My phone was down by my leg, so he tossed it to me. I stood and paced the floor. I knew it was something dealing with my family, and I just prayed to God it wasn't anything too bad that would leave me devastated because I'd been ignoring her calls.

"Asha?" Gary, the dispatcher, answered. Most officers had a great relationship with the dispatchers. We all worked together to get through shifts.

"Yes? Everything okay?"

"We just got a domestic call from your sister. Since the call came to me, I decided to call you instead of any other officer. I remember you asking me to always call you if I was to ever get a call from Arielle."

"Thanks, Gary." I hung up the phone and rapidly dressed.

I wasn't even thinking, just dressing. "What happened?" Demaris asked, looking worried.

"I don't know. It must be bad for Arielle to call the cops. I have to go." I made sure my gun was on safety and put it back in my holster.

"I'll meet you there."

"Baby, please. No. I got this."

"You sure?" His keys were in his hand, and he was already tossing his shirt over his head.

"I'm sure."

"Give me some love," he said, walking over to me and leaning down for a kiss.

"Muah."

"Let me know what's going on when you get there."

"Okay, I love you." I rushed out the front door. Break time was over.

I got into the car and didn't blast my sirens like I wanted to. Then other police would follow me. I didn't need that right now.

I tried to call Sway, but she didn't answer, and neither did Tweety. I even tried to call Spin, but she didn't answer either.

It was always something with Mama Crystal. Always. Before I even got there, I knew it had something to do with her being bad on drugs again. Arielle never, and I mean *never*, called the cops under any circumstances.

Fuck! I hit the steering wheel as I sped through the Dallas streets. *Why didn't I fucking answer?*

When I turned onto my street, I saw a cop car already there. To make matters worse, it was Dennis. Before getting out, I called Gary's cellular back. "I'm sorry, Asha. He called and asked if everything was okay," Gary said. "He must've heard me channel you and tell you to call me."

"So, he took it upon himself to get all up in my business?" I asked as I made sure all my equipment was on me.

"I only told him it was a call from your little sister. He pressed for the address, and I said I didn't know, but he mentioned tampering with a potential investigation, so I had to give him the address. Please forgive me."

"I'm not mad at you at all. Trust me. I'll handle this shit." I hung up the phone and slammed the door once I got out of the car.

I saw Arielle talking to Dennis, which pissed me off even more. He stood with his notebook writing something down.

"What the fuck are you doing?" I asked him, snatching Arielle behind me.

"I'm doing my job." He looked confused, which offended me.

I was about to go off until I saw Arielle's clothes ripped and Mama Crystal with a bloody lip. I pulled her away so Dennis couldn't hear.

"What happened?" Arielle's eye was already turning blue. "What the fuck happened?" I asked again when she didn't answer.

"Three days ago, I told Sway that Ma was on drugs bad again. She's selling everything she can touch, and the money y'all give her goes to drugs and to her new boyfriend. So, Sway poured all her drugs down the toilet."

"She's been on drugs."

"No, it's bad again. She's doing Black Tar."

"Are you serious?" I asked as Arielle cried and hugged me, slamming her face into my chest.

"Yes. Since Sway flushed most of it away, Mama has been trying to get more, but she's all out of favors and money, so she called Ski Man over here and told him I would suck his dick for two hundred dollars."

Ski Man was a local drug dealer who had to be in his late twenties. He wasn't much older than me. He was known to accept sexual favors in place of money.

"He hit you?"

"Yes, because I told him, no, and apparently Ma had already used the drugs he gave her for me sucking his dick. He beat me up, and when Mama tried to stop him, he beat her up. He keeps threatening to come back and shoot the house up."

"What the fuck?"

Ski Man was one of the ones who came up with us. He knew Arielle was our little sister. The fact that he still tried that bull had me on ten. I jerked my head over to Mama Crystal and gave her a death stare. She knew she would have to deal with all of us. Arielle was off-limits. Period. That's been understood since she was a baby.

"I'm sorry for calling the cops, but Ski Man scares me. He keeps telling Ma he's going to kidnap me and kill me."

"That's the least of your worries. Trust me. Listen, have you told the male officer anything?"

"No, Asha. I promise. I just kept asking for you."

"And what he say?"

"He said it would be a conflict of interest for you to work this case."

"Go in the house," I told her, and she did as I said.

Mama Crystal sat on the porch smoking a cigarette. She knew she'd fucked up. It was written all over her face.

"Get that man from in front of my house," Mama Crystal said.

I wanted to light into her ass, but I couldn't with him right there.

I charged over to Dennis just as he was about to talk on the radio. "What are you doing?"

"Reporting child abuse. That little girl is clearly in danger."

"Listen, this doesn't need to be an investigation. We're not getting outside cops or CPS involved."

"Technically, you aren't supposed to be working this case. This is a family issue, making it a conflict of interest."

"Yeah, I know. But this is my family. My sister can just stay with me until everything is sorted out. She has people who love her."

"Like who? You and Sway?" He rolled his eyes.

Now I knew he'd really taken that picture from my house. He only brought up Sway because she was the only one who still looked the same, just older.

"I don't know what you're talking about or what that has to do with anything, but you need to stay out of my fucking business."

"I don't know. Maybe I wouldn't be in your business if you would answer my calls and texts."

"I don't have time for this. Leave my mom's house."

"Are you calling this in?"

"Leave, Dennis. I promise I'll call you today, but for now, I need to handle this."

He backed away slowly. "I'll be waiting for that call."

"I bet you will."

After he left, I stormed over to Ma and made her go inside so I could have privacy for the way I was about to get heated.

Once inside, I got a full view of the scene. It looked like a tornado had come through and messed everything up. I then began to wonder just how bad he beat them because blood was everywhere.

"Whose nose was leaking?" I asked.

"Mine," Mama Crystal said.

I started to touch her face, but Arielle grabbed my hand to stop me.

"What?"

"Ma just found out she has AIDS. Use gloves." She handed me rubber gloves after putting hers on. She also had some bleach spray.

"Excuse me?" I couldn't have heard her right. But the way Ma walked away from me and sat on the couch with her head down, I knew it was true. "Dirty needles? So, you really back into that shit again, huh?"

"I know I fucked up. This is all Sway's fucking fault. If she wouldn't have flushed my shit, then—"

"Then what?" I got in her face. "Then what?! You wouldn't have solicited your daughter to a predator? Is that what you about to tell me? Huh? Ma, I swear before God!"

"Asha, come on."

I didn't notice I was so far in her face until Arielle pulled me back.

"I need help."

"You damn right you need help. Arielle, go pack as much as you can. We'll come back and get the rest."

Ma stood up like she wanted to resist. "Sitcho'ass down before I tear this place up more than it already is. You *think* Ski got on your ass."

"Well, he saying he gon' blow the house up."

"Don't you worry about him. He will be dealt with before the night."

"Why everything gotta be violence with my children? Huh?"

"What else we gon' do, Mama? Huh?"

She shrugged. "Fuck it. Just fuck it."

"You're getting help, and you're getting it today. I don't care what you say. You're going to rehab. I'm not doing this shit with you no more."

"What rehab gon' do about this disease? Huh?"

"They can get you started on some medication. It's not a death sentence like it used to be."

"Y'all got me fucked up." She stood and walked toward the front door. "I'm the mama. Y'all ain't my damn mama." She walked out, slamming the door behind her.

"I'm ready." Asha was packed with two large roller suitcases. "This everything. Mama sold everything else. I also got some money from a job I did for Sway and from when she took me to get ice cream."

I took one of the bags. "Cool."

Once we got in the car, I drove off and asked, "Did he rape you?"

"No. He tried, but I fought him off with the mace you gave me. That's what pissed him off."

"Fucking Ski Man." I couldn't wait to talk to Demaris.

"Please don't make me go back. Even if she does get help. I don't want to go back, Asha, please."

"I would never ever send you back there. Not after this. I can't believe Sway even let you stay after she found all that out." I shook my head.

"In Sway's defense, she had a lot on her plate. It's a lot she hasn't told you guys about what she's going through. She thought she was helping by pouring the drugs out."

"Fuck that. Sway grew up with Mama Crystal when she was worse than this. She knows that woman gets desperate when she's out of drugs. She fucking knew better. Putting you at risk was unacceptable."

"I don't know what to do." She looked so uneasy and stressed. Man, I hated this.

"It's not for you to figure out. Let the adults handle it. All you need to worry about is being a smart, talented, and beautiful teenager. That's all. Worry about enjoying your summer with your friends. No, you not gon' be like us. You ain't about to spend the summer taking care of Ma and trying to get money for school. No. Fuck no."

I went and bought her some food for the day and some snacks. I then went to clock out early and switched over to my car.

When I got to my apartment, Demaris was already gone. I got Arielle settled into the guest bedroom. Afterward, I showered and put some clothes on. It was almost five, so I knew where Ski Man was; somewhere in front of the Kliff Klub posted and gambling. Before leaving, I made sure my gun was on me. Demaris wasn't answering, so I texted him and told him where I was on my way to, just in case he saw the messages.

Being that the Kliff Klub was an after-hours spot, people were outside bumping music and chilling on top of trunks. I didn't see him at first until someone said his name. He was over by the edge of the street, closer to the car wash.

Once I zeroed in on him, I swerved in front of his car and hopped out. His boys grabbed their guns, but he laughed and said, "Y'all good. This bitch thinks she finna check me about her hoe ass sister."

"You put your hands on her. She's a child, Ski. You're a grown ass man!"

"Mane, that lil' hoe know she be fuckin'. You know it too."

"So, that means she obligated to fuck you?"

He leaned against his old school Chevy with a too-big shirt on and some baggy jeans. He dressed like it was still 2006 when guys wore tall tees. He even wore the king braids with beads. Ski Man hung around a bunch of teenagers who protected him. Everyone our age knew he was full of shit.

"I ain't say that. All I'm saying is I was promised some time, and I ain't get it. Then the lil' bitch pepper sprayed me."

"Because you tried to rape her!"

"Say it again and watch I slap you."

"Bitch ass nigga, you ain't scaring me."

He dropped his cup and charged at me. I swerved to the side

and used my foot to trip him. As he fell over, I kneed him in the nuts and used that opportunity to get him into a choke hold.

One of his crash dummy niggas tried to draw down on me, but I pulled my weapon and pointed it at Ski Man's head. "Anybody else, and I swear to God I'm sending a bullet through his skull. Try me."

Everyone stood down. "Now you listen to me, you bitch ass nigga. If I ever catch you around my family members again, you dead. You know how the fuck we get down, nigga."

He spat at the ground. "Fuck you, bitch."

I choked him until he couldn't breathe and cried for me to stop. "Okay! Okay!"

"Got it?"

"I got it."

Before I let him go, I took the butt of the gun and hit him on the left side of his temple three times, knocking him out cold.

"Don't look so alarmed," I said while everyone watched in panic as he fell to the ground. "Other than a terrible headache, he'll be fine." I backed away to my car with my weapon drawn on him. "I'm leaving now. Anyone try and stop me, he dies."

After getting into the car, I burned rubber out of there. Ski Man was crazy but not crazier than us. I knew we wouldn't have any problems after this. He hated to be embarrassed or shown out. It was his weakness.

Since it was still dark, and I knew Delyle's club was just about closing, I took a chance to see if I could catch him alone. By the time I got there, it should've been empty.

When I got to his club, it was only a few cars parked outside. "Please be here," I said to myself as I grabbed my keys out of the ignition and went inside.

"We're closed, honey," one of the bartenders said to me as she dried a glass.

"I'm here for Delyle."

"He isn't here."

"You sure?"

"Look, honey, I said he isn't here. Leave before I get you tossed out."

I didn't have the energy to argue, so I just prepared to leave.

The phone rang next to her. "Yes? Okay. Got it. Sending her up now," she said. "I'm sorry. Come with me." She walked me over to a janitor's closet. It beeped and let us inside. "Elevators are that way. Press the top floor." She closed the door and left.

I did as I was told, shocked by how well put together everything was in there.

Once at the top floor, the door opened, and my eyes laid on the most beautiful loft setup I had ever seen. One so beautiful that it shouldn't have existed. It overlooked the entire club with a wall length window that was clearly tinted. On the inside, I could see it all, but on the outside, one wouldn't know this was a loft. It looked to be part of the decoration.

"You caught me just as I was about to leave." He showed me to my seat at the personal bar.

"I'm so sorry for catching you like this. I just feel like you're a pretty level headed guy, and I wanted to know your thoughts on a situation."

"Trust me, it's fine. What's the situation? Want a glass of wine to take the edge off?"

I nodded. "Yes. Please and thank you."

He slid me a wine glass and poured red wine into it. "So, what's up?"

"I don't even know where to start." I took a huge gulp of wine. Instantly, I felt a whole lot better. "Oh, that's good."

"Start anywhere."

"I just had a situation with my mom and sister."

I broke down everything to him, down to every small detail. I made sure I didn't leave out anything, not even the part about pistol-whipping Ski Man before leaving.

He leaned against the cabinet across from me. With his arms folded, he said, "I don't think that was a good idea."

"What?"

"What you did. You did it in front of everyone who looks up to him. We live in the era of social media, too, so now things are worse. Now, everyone knows that he's potentially a child molester, and he also was beaten horrendously by a woman. He's going to want some revenge. He may even take it too far just to outdo you. I say finish him."

I shook my head and blew him off. "Nonsense. Trust me, I have known him since I was a child. We all grew up together."

"That could make it worse. Where is your sister?"

"With me. He's not going after her."

"That's the first person he will go after. He now knows your weakness. He knows you can fend for yourself. He only hangs around kids because he knows people his age can handle him. He preys on the weak."

"I know what I'm dealing with."

He shook his head and grinned. "Okay. Just keep your eyes open. You may think he's a pussy, but now he's a humiliated pussy with a lot to prove."

I changed the subject. "What I really wanted advice on was Dennis," I lied.

I just didn't want him telling me something I knew wouldn't happen. Ski was a straight pussy bitch. One had to know how he was growing up to understand why I said that. Niggas put him in a blender all the time.

"What about Dennis?"

"I'm sure by now you know about us. I know he's told you."

"Are you asking about Demaris or Dennis?"

"How did you know?"

"I saw the cameras from the back of the club that day. What do you want to know?"

"I want to know if I should tell Dennis."

"I don't involve myself with other people's matters of the heart. I think you're a grown woman with your own choices to make. You do as you feel in a time like this."

"I just don't want to hurt either of them."

"Who do you love? Or do you love them both?"

"I have come to realize that I love Demaris, but I was overly attracted to Dennis. I liked the way he looked physically."

"And Demaris?"

"Demaris is nearly as attractive as Dennis, but I love him. He's good for me. He wants what's best for me. He's a little crazy, but it can be worked on."

He laughed. "He's just like his dad was. Very headstrong and passionate about who and what they chose to love."

"I heard you and their dad were close. How was he as a person?"

"He was very loyal. Loyal to a fault sometimes." He wasn't smiling anymore. He went down memory lane, and the road seemed to be a dark one with a little light. "He was ruthless but not to those he loved. Not at all. If he loved a woman or anyone, they could fuck him over a million times, and he'd still be there to catch them whenever they fell. I would always tell him his heart would be the death of him, and ultimately, it was."

"Was he as crazy as his son?"

"Oh, no. See, their dad was a thinker. He calculated every move. He was a dangerous man but not nearly as dangerous as Demaris. Demaris is hot-tempered, and judging by the tape, you know just how far he's willing to go when he feels wronged."

"That's not even the worst part," I said, thinking of the cop that he killed on the way to me.

"All in all, Demaris is a great guy unless someone is on his bad side. He loves too hard, but it's hereditary. He doesn't give up on people, so he expects the same in return."

"That's an argument we had. I want to be with him, but...." I cut myself off and thought of another way to explain. "You ever hopped into a situation thinking, *this isn't going to end well*?" I asked.

"More times than I care to admit. Sure."

"That's how I feel. What if we have a small disagreement, and he wants to kill me for it?"

"Nah, it would be more than a small disagreement. Give him more credit than that."

"What if he ever catches me cheating? You know? Something so minor."

"If you think cheating is minor, maybe you should end this with Demaris right now." He wasn't smiling, and he looked me dead in the eyes.

"Yeah?"

"Yes."

"I wouldn't cheat. Let me get that part clear. I was just asking, worst case scenario."

"I think you should ask him all these things before you two go forward with this. Although Demaris can act out of rage when he's hurt, I don't think he's the one you need to worry about."

"Who?"

"What do you think Dennis will say when he finds out? You think he's going to go on about his merry way and wish you two well?"

"No, I don't."

"What do you think will happen?"

"He's been low-key threatening to expose my affiliation with my gang."

"Your focus shouldn't be on pissing Demaris off. Demaris has loyalty and rage."

"And Dennis just has rage?" I asked.

"I didn't agree to that."

"But you didn't disagree."

"You have bigger fish to fry. It's neither Demaris nor Dennis. It's the child lover. Once he's done licking his wounds, he will come after your sister."

"I think you're wise, but when it comes to this, I think I got it. We've done worse to tougher people. He got the picture."

He glanced down to the bar area. Sitting at the table was Terry. "A hard head makes a soft ass," he said while gathering his things.

"You know Terry?"

He smirked. "He's my son. You couldn't tell?"

"Wow. No, I had no idea. He's dating my friend, but nobody knows but us."

"Sway thinks he killed her ex? Right?"

"I see he tells you a lot."

"That's my boy. It's not much I don't know." He led me to the elevator and let me inside before him.

"So, do you know if he killed Houston?"

He brushed his nose with the knuckle of his index finger. "I don't appreciate the audacity you have to ask me something like that involving my son. I know I've made you feel comfortable, but don't ever ask me anything like that again. In fact, don't mention my son to me. We have no reason to discuss him." He held his hand out when the elevator stopped on the first floor.

"I'm so sorry, Mr. Delyle. It was the wine. I truly didn't mean any disrespect." I meant my apology. "I don't even know what I was thinking." Like really, what was I expecting him to say?

"It's fine. Enjoy the rest of your day and get some rest."

"What's up, Asha?" Terry nodded at me on the way out.

"Nothing much."

"You good?"

"I'm straight. Y'all be easy," I said as I walked out.

It wasn't until Delyle locked the door behind me that I realized he'd nicely put me out.

TERRY
LOVE AND DESTRUCTION

I leaned back in the chair and nodded at the door. "What you up to with Asha?"

"You think I'm up to something?"

"You're always up to something. I know you don't just like her personality, and that's why she just left your loft." I laughed.

"That's exactly what it is, actually. She's a nice girl. You know? Got her head on straight."

"Definitely agree on that." I left it alone.

One thing I loved about my dad is that he never lied. Whenever he said something, better believe he meant it. We had our ups and downs, but having him in my corner always made life much easier for my siblings and me.

He was there for all six of us, right or wrong, even after he left my mother. There was never a time I needed him and he wasn't there. Ever. Whether it was street shit or just regular life, he was there. Even if we both were hard to love at times. My dad taught me everything I know, but sometimes I did veer off path.

I'd put him through a lot. I used to think my younger brother, Loc, and I were a disappointment to him because my older four siblings were all successful and married with degrees behind them. Then, there I was, in the streets. Though I was out there bad, I didn't think I was worse than my younger brother, Loc. If one was to meet Loc first and then our dad, you'd have no idea he belonged to Delyle.

"What brings you here? You need advice, too?"

"Ahh, who else been asking my old man for advice?"

He let out a hearty laugh. "I've been feeling like a catholic priest these days. It's all love, though."

"That's why Asha was here?"

He grinned. "You don't need to worry about why she was here. Just know she was here."

"You got it, old man."

"I look younger than you."

"Sheeeit, I look better than you," I joked back.

"You took after me. That's the only reason women find you attractive."

"People been saying I look like Mama lately."

"You got some of her features." His face turned serious. "So, what's up?"

"I think I fucked up."

"What you mean?"

"With my girl."

"Which one."

"I only got one."

"I still can't believe you did that." My dad, for some reason, wasn't all the way fond of Spin yet.

"I love her."

"You pity her."

"That too," I admitted. "I'm the reason she's going through what she's going through. I do feel fucked up about that. I just think I've bitten off more than I can chew this time."

"I've told you that from the very beginning before you made the decision. We talked about this."

"I know." I dragged my hands down my face.

"She's going to find out eventually."

"I don't think so."

"You also thought her and Crystal would never cross paths."

He had a point there. "I know."

"I would say she's smart, and eventually she'll figure it out, but that's not the case. She's envious and can't be trusted. She will betray you out of spite."

"Then I'll kill her."

"Spin isn't like Crystal. Crystal dealt with her heartbreak like a woman. She kicked her wounds in silence. She had class about it. Spin is going to scorch the earth."

"It was the only way to put a halt to this fucking war Sway started. Dad, I got too much shit going on in the streets to be beefing with bitches."

"Then maybe you shouldn't have killed her brother."

"It was an accident. You know that. I was trying to hit the nigga on the side of him."

"This is why I've always told you to walk down your opponent. Shooting in a crowd is very cowardly."

"I could never catch his pussy ass anywhere, so the day I did, I took my chance. If I had walked him down, then the entire crowd would've pointed me out in a lineup within hours."

"Or you could've just followed him from the party like I would've done."

"That party had just started and was going to be happening for hours. I ain't have time for that."

"This is why patience is a virtue. Now the wrong man is dead, and you're fucking his sister. To make matters worse, you've convinced yourself that you're in love with her."

"What if I am?"

"You're not, but if you keep at it, you can fall in love."

I sighed. He was right. The more time I spent with Spin, the more I fell for the type of person she was. Usually, I wouldn't go for a girl like her, but she brought something out of me that I hated to love. Some would call it toxic.

"She's fun."

"She might be. Crystal is safe."

"She's also boring. She made her whole life about me. What's the fun in that? I never want anyone to be that much into me to the point that they make their entire life about me."

He gave me the eye like a father. His hand slightly lifted from the table, and he pointed at me like I was in trouble. "The very thing you didn't like about Crystal will be the same thing you miss. You mark my words."

"I'll just pray to God that you're wrong. I love it here."

"Toxicity gets old, son. By the time you're close to thirty, you just want peace. Have you gone to check on Crystal like I told you to?"

I knew he was about to be disappointed when I said what I was about to say. "I can't face her. I just can't do it."

He shook his head. "With other people, I don't involve myself in relationships. But with my children, there are no limits. If I told you to check on her, I didn't say it for my own health."

"You sound like Mama." I peeped the bartender staring at me. She was fine as hell. "She had enough support. Mama wouldn't let her out of her sight."

"Out of all the love she had, it was yours she wanted. Your comfort was the only comfort she wanted. I can almost guarantee you that." He pulled out a cigar. "It's not too late."

"What if she slams the door in my face?"

"She won't."

"Man, why are you so heavy on this?"

"I take loyalty very seriously, and she has a lot of that for you. Just for you to turn around and not be there for her when she needs you the most. I raised you better."

"You go be there for her then."

The look he gave me was similar to the look he gave me before I got shot, and he told me I was heading down a road to get myself shot. It was a stern look. "Excuse me?"

I sighed. "I'm just saying. I feel like if I go, she will turn me away. Besides, I'm with Spin, so I can't just go over there."

"I'm going to say this, and then I've spoken my peace. Spin

seems to be reckless, sloppy even, and that's never good. It's going to cost you. She'll burst sooner or later. You got time, son. But you like to live on the dangerous side."

Changing the subject, I said, "Mama is gone again." Not only did his demeanor change, but his energy changed. I felt it.

Once upon a time, he loved my mother. I truly believed that. One doesn't just give a woman six kids and not love her. I often wondered what she did to break his heart, causing him to break hers. She was never quite the same after he left. That's when the drugs started.

"Find her," was all he said.

I always wanted to know what made my dad fall for someone like my mom. Or maybe back then, he was a different person, and she chose not to grow when he did. I didn't know. All I knew for sure was he completely denounced my mother, leaving her destroyed.

"It's been almost twenty years since the last time you spoke to her."

"Make me understand your point."

"She needs you."

"She needs help, not me."

"Help doesn't work with her. You know that. We've all tried. All six of us." Even my oldest brother, who told people he didn't have a mother, tried to help Icis.

Years ago, for an entire month, he took leave from work and came to stay with her and help her. She manipulated him into thinking she was getting better and cleaned his bank account once she had his trust again. Dad replaced everything she stole, but the money wasn't the problem. It was the principle. She hurt him deeply. He hadn't talked to her since that day.

"I honestly don't know what to tell you, son. I'm not going around her. Not because of any old vendettas, but because if I do, your mother isn't going to let me go. She's going to take me helping her as me wanting her, and she's going to fuck up a lot of things. I don't have the time nor patience for her recklessness."

"I won't keep pressuring you about it." I glanced over at the bar to find the bartender giving me the eyes again. "She loves you, Dad."

"This I know."

"Who's the bartender?"

Without turning to see who I was talking about, he said, "You will not fuck anyone who works for me. It's a major conflict of interest waiting to happen."

I smirked. "She's looking like she wants the kid."

"Well, *the kid* better keep looking, and that's it."

We talked for a few minutes more and parted ways. Talking to him always made me feel balanced. I didn't take all his advice. I was just waiting for the day to prove him wrong, and I really hoped he was wrong about Spin. I really cared about her.

So many times, I just wanted to break down and tell her how it was an accident, and I didn't mean to kill her brother, but I knew that would be the worst mistake of my life so far. So, I kept it all inside.

On the way back to Ft. Worth, I grabbed some food. Shortly after, I headed to my mom's house to see if I could find any clues as to where she might be. I hated when she did this disappearing shit. Most of the time, she would be in jail or a hospital, but I had already checked those. She wasn't there.

Crystal wasn't home yet; her car wasn't outside. That was good. I didn't want to run into her. No matter what my dad said, I just didn't feel like she was a good fit for me. We weren't into the same things. We were complete opposites that didn't attract.

Mama's house was clean, and I knew she didn't clean it. Crystal kept her house clean to keep her from stepping on old needles. She wanted Mama to be able to see where she was stepping.

As I was in the kitchen, going through old mail and bills, I noticed the dog wasn't in his doghouse, and no food was in his bowl.

"Not again," I said and tossed the papers down on the table.

The sun was just now coming up, making it another day she'd been sleeping in the doghouse.

If I said I wasn't afraid of what I might have found, I would be lying. I always told myself that one of these days, I was going to find her not alive.

"Mama." I pulled her leg, dragging her soiled body out of the doghouse.

She reeked of shit, piss, outside, and dog. I saw her breathing, so I knew she was alive. All I needed to do was wake her enough to where I could at least see her eyes and what state they were in.

I grabbed the water hose and washed as much junk off of her as I could. It wasn't until the water hit her face and almost drowned her that she woke up. Her eyes were beautiful and brown, no red in sight, which was a great sign. Her once silky, beautiful hair was now coarse and dry. Mama's beautiful caramel skin was flawless still. All she needed was a year of being sober, and she would shave twenty years off her looks. She would look young, just like my dad. Now, she looked her age.

"Stop! Okay! I'm up!" She used her hands to try and shield her face from the water.

I used the hose to put water in the dog's bowl and put food in the other one while Mama gathered her energy to stand to her feet. "How long was I out?" She took her drenched clothes off.

"Days."

She laughed it off. "Oh, that's not good. I was damn near in hibernation."

I didn't respond to that. "I'll run you a bath. You stink."

She saw the look of disappointment on my face and frowned, trying to grab my hand as I walked by her. I jerked away. "Terry, please."

I walked to her bathroom to run her a hot bath. I thought the morphine was working, but Morphine didn't do this. It was heroin.

After running her bath water, I helped her inside and sat on the arm of the tub. She lay back just enough to get her lips wet in the water and blew bubbles. "Was I out that long, huh?"

"Long enough for Crystal to worry."

Her eyes beamed with joy. "You saw her?"

"Diamond ran away and went over to her house. She brought her back on her lunch break and told me you were gone." I used the towel to squeeze warm water on her hair.

"You know you dead wrong for not checking up on that girl after her brother died. And don't say you ain't know he was dead. You saw the news, and I texted you."

"I can't face her, Mama."

"It's easy. You just go over and sit down to talk like a regular damn human being."

"When she came to my place and saw my new girl, the look in her eyes hurt me, Mama. I ain't know I could feel that way."

"Because you love her."

"I do. I didn't say I didn't, but I just don't think she and I are meant for each other. I've hurt her too much. She might hate me and want to get some get back one day."

She blew me off. "This generation ain't worth a damn."

"How so?"

"Y'all too busy trying to wife up sneaky links."

"Who a sneaky link? Not mine."

"Chile, I heard about her. She in the streets harder than you, and you gon' sit here in my face and tell me my baby ain't the one for you. Let me guess, she's too boring?"

"It's not that. I just don't think I deserve her. She deserves someone better than me. I don't want her trying to modify herself to my liking."

"You still wrong."

"You sound like Dad."

She glared at me from the corner of her eye. "You've seen him?"

"Just left."

"He ask about me?"

"He was concerned about your well being."

"So, he didn't ask about me," she said. I didn't respond. "You two are so much alike but so different."

"Everyone says that."

"That man sure can hold a grudge."

I never asked exactly what went down between the two because, whatever it was, it was enough to make him walk away after all those years. To be honest, I was afraid to find out what happened. That's why I stayed out of it.

"Come on, let's get you out." I gave her a towel and let her go to the room alone to get dressed.

While she was dressing, I caught a glimpse of myself in the mirror and had many flashbacks. It almost felt like the man in the mirror wasn't me. It was hard to even tell who I was looking at. I was better than how I had been.

That man in the mirror wasn't me. All I saw was love and destruction.

After mama got dressed, she ate a sandwich and snuggled into bed. "You take good care of me," she said as I sat on the edge of the bed.

"You took good care of me all my life."

"You love me?" she asked.

I knew where she was going with this. "Yes."

"She should be off by now. Go over and check on her. It's the least you can do."

"Mama..." I sighed. "I can only be me, Mama. Me going over there right now ain't me."

"I can't even begin to explain how disappointed I am. I know your father feels the same way."

"He does. But this ain't y'all life. It's mine. What if she turns me away? Then what?"

"She won't."

"You seem so sure. I hurt her, and I hurt her bad."

"It's called unconditional love." She grabbed my face. "The type of love I have for you."

"I'm scared of the way she might look at me. She might see the flaws in me."

"She saw them a long time ago, far before you saw hers. The only difference is, she saw your flaws and loved you. You saw hers and left her."

"That cut me deep. Don't do me like that."

"It's time to man up and face the music."

"Okay."

"Okay, what?"

"I'm going to see about her."

"When?"

"Whenever I see her. She's not here right now."

Just as I said that, Mama smiled and blew me off. "Now, go wait on her. I need to rest."

CRYSTAL
A TOXIC ASS NIGGA

Pulling up to the house, the first thing I saw was Terry's car. Seeing his car still made my heart jump. Even though I promised my brother I would leave Terry and me in the past, I wasn't quite sure I knew how. He still held a place right in the middle of my heart. He was above all, beneath none. I just wished he felt the same way.

The fact that ambulances weren't there let me know Icis was fine. I would check on her after I woke up. He would be gone by then. I knew he wanted to avoid me, so I would make it easy for him.

Soon as I opened the door, there he was, sitting on the couch. His face was rested in his palms, so he hadn't noticed me yet. I wasn't slow. He was only there because his mama wanted him there. I could tell because he still hadn't noticed me standing there. I tossed my keys on the table to get his attention and took my shoes off.

He still didn't lift his head. "Morning, Crystal."

"Morning. Did you get lost?" I asked as I headed into the kitchen to take some meds for a horrible headache that I'd been nursing all night.

"Nah, I used the key and walked in so I could wait."

"Glad to see you still have a spare key."

"Can we talk without the attitude?" he asked, still with his face in his palms.

"I'm sorry. Would you like something to drink?"

He shook his head. "Icis is okay."

"I figured. Where was she?"

He finally lifted his head and leaned back on the couch. "The doghouse."

I swallowed the pills and washed them down with water. "Seriously?"

"Yeah. She's okay now, though. I don't think the morphine is working anymore."

"Clearly. I think it's time for rehab, Terry." I placed the glass down.

"I didn't come here to talk about Icis. Icis is fine right now and sleeping peacefully."

"So, what did you come to talk about?"

"We can talk about me first." He stood and removed his chain and watch, placing them on top of the TV. This meant he would be staying a while. I was pleased with that.

"What about you?"

He sat back down and sighed. "Crystal, I'm so sorry about how I've been treating you, ma."

Just those few words changed the course of my morning and probably my life. I didn't know he had this in him. I had a new view of him. First, I lost faith in him, and now I was gaining it back. No matter who made him come, he was hard to persuade, so he came because he wanted to.

"Don't say words you don't mean." I cleared my throat, trying to hide the fact that my voice was cracking.

"I mean it. You can ask me anything you want to know, and I promise my honesty. You deserve that."

"You mean it?"

He rubbed the empty spot next to him, motioning for me to come and sit down. "Yes. Come here."

I walked over and sat down. He grabbed both hands and gazed into my eyes. He meant it all. I could see the regret and sorrow.

"Did you cheat on me with Spin?"

"No. I left so I wouldn't cheat."

"I saw on Facebook that her brother is... was Houston. The guy killed at that party."

"Yes."

"Yes, what?" I asked.

"Yes, that's the man I killed on accident. I met her a little before that, but after I found out that it was her brother who was killed, I pushed the issue and made her my girlfriend. I felt like I owed her that."

"So, I was right?"

"About what?"

"You're with her out of pity?"

"I also have deep feelings for her."

"How do you think this will end? Huh? You think she's going to stop trying to find who killed her brother?"

"I know, but it was an accident. You know that."

"So, you think once you explain it was an accident, everything will be all fine and dandy? Right?"

"I don't know what I think."

"It's not going to end well. You know that."

"If it turns out bad, then it turns out bad. I don't know how to handle it yet because I don't know how this will go. I don't know how she will react."

"The right thing to do is leave her. Don't fuck her out of a chance to leave with some dignity. I always hear rumors about her and that gang she's with. They don't call her Spin for nothing, I heard."

He smiled like he was proud to have a shooter as a girlfriend. "I already know. Is it me you're worried about? Or her?"

"It's you. What if she finds out you killed her brother while you're asleep one day? And she kills you while you're resting?

Then what? What about me? What about Icis? What about Loc? What about the rest of your siblings? Do you even think of anyone other than yourself?"

"I've thought about all of that."

Tired of talking about Spin and a reaction she may or may not have, I asked, "Have you eaten?"

He shook his head. "Nah. You want to cook for me?"

I smiled and rubbed my thighs before standing. "Steak and eggs?"

"You know it."

He walked over, sat at the dinner table, and watched me but not in a sad way. More like a gentle way. He was thinking. I wanted to ask what was on his mind, but I knew if I did, he would shut down pretty fast about it.

"I saw on Facebook people posting the memorial you out together for Earth's birthday. That was nice of you."

"That was my mans. Least I could do. It was his baby mama's idea. I just paid for it. Her giving me the credit was cool, I guess."

"His children looked extremely happy to be there."

"I saw that. It made me feel good."

"Why didn't you go?" I asked as I prepared the food to cook.

"Ma, I've been to enough funerals and memorials this year and last year to last a lifetime. If it ain't the police killing us, it's us killing ourselves."

"You play a big role."

"I never drilled anybody that didn't push me. I had to be pushed."

"True."

He was right. That's what he was known for, actually. He didn't bother anyone who didn't come looking for him. It was usually easy for him to stay out of drama for that reason right there. Most rivals respected him enough to stay out of his way, and he would, in return, stay out of their way. It was the way he moved.

"Working the ER, I see so much. I'm always so afraid that one night I might go into work and see you being pumped and under the knife to stay alive."

"I wouldn't do you like that. I promise."

"Please don't do me like that. I already lost my brother. You get on my nerves, but I would go crazy if anything happened to you." I grabbed a glass and a container of orange juice with no pulp. I poured us both some and put extra ice in his. There was something on his mind. I could tell. "What's wrong?"

It was like he didn't notice me standing there. "Huh?"

"You're worried about what may happen if she finds out, huh?"

"I am."

"I don't want to keep saying the same thing over and over, but for your sake and hers, try to go about this in a way nobody gets hurt. She loves you, but we both know how thin the line is between love and hate."

"How do we both know?" He drank some juice. "You think I hate you?"

"It feels like it sometimes."

"I will never hate you. I actually love you very much."

That made my heart smile. "That's shocking."

"Why?"

"You won't even let me tell you how much I love you without cutting me off."

"It ain't like that. I just don't want you to feel like I'm playing with your feelings."

"I wouldn't feel like that. It just don't hurt to say it back."

"I love you, Crystal."

I placed the food on the plate and slid it to him. "It's hot."

"You're not hungry?" He grabbed his fork and prepared to dive in.

"I already ate at work."

I sat down across from him and gave him silence so he could get into the food. He ate like he hadn't had time to eat. "I love the way you make my eggs."

"Fluffy?"

"With love." He burst into laughter. "Look, you was about to risk it all over there."

I tossed a napkin at him. "Clown. I'm about to shower. I'll be back."

I was starting to smell the blood from a patient last night. It still lingered in my nose. I showered like twice a day because of that.

While I was in the shower, I thought about how easy it was for Terry to be back on my mind. I thought I knew him. Hell, I couldn't blame him because I thought I knew myself too. Turns out, we do grow every second of the day. We grow into whole ass new people.

This man chose not to come around when I needed him the most, and all I could think about was him touching me. I wanted him to caress my body and kiss me. It would feel so nice for him to tell me how he messed up and wanted to be with me again.

Judging by the way he had just laughed at his own joke, buddy had tossed me into the friend zone. That was never fun. I wanted him to stay but was more so ready for him to leave. If I couldn't have him, I didn't want to be around him much longer. I was afraid I might break.

The bathroom door opened, startling me. I grabbed my breast. "Terry, you scared the hell out of me."

He dropped the lid on the toilet and sat down. "I've seen everything you have to offer. No need to hide."

Dropping my hands, I said, "I know. Not like you want me anyway."

"I want you."

He said it so smooth and quick that I didn't notice he'd said it. I had to do a double back. "Huh?"

"I want you. I just don't want to hurt you." He turned his phone off and stood up, pulling his shirt over his head and tossing it on the floor. What was he doing? "Can I touch you?" He neared the shower, removing the rest of his clothes.

A cat must have had my tongue. I couldn't speak at first. He stood there with his dick hanging, semi-hard. This was happening. I'd been wanting this—needing this. "Sure."

He waited for my permission and stepped into the shower behind me. "Can I kiss you?"

I nodded, holding my towel for dear life against my chest. He leaned down and kissed my neck, pulling away with a bite. A gentle bite. "Terry."

"Talk to me." He grabbed my hands, squeezing them, as he licked the back of my neck. "You don't want to talk now?" he asked.

"I do."

"Have I told you I love you?"

"Yes."

"Have I said it enough?" he asked as he bent me over with my hands gripping the soap holder hanging from the shower faucet.

"No." I moaned as he entered me from behind.

His strong hands gripped my waist as he towered over me, watching my facial expressions. "I love you so much, Crystal."

"You mean it?" I asked.

He pushed his dick so deep into me. "I mean it."

"I love you."

"How much?"

Instead of responding, I moaned. He then went deeper into my pussy. "Talk to me, love."

"I love you more than anything."

"You'll do anything for me?"

"Yes. I'll do anything for you," I cried out.

"Let me hear you scream."

"Fuck." He felt so good to me.

"Let me hear you scream my name."

"Terry!"

"I'm yo' daddy."

"Daddy!"

"Yeah. Give me all that. I feel you cumming on daddy dick."

He pounded me harder and held me tighter as I indeed came all over daddy's dick.

I caught my breath as he pried my hands away from the soap holder. After my hands were down, he picked me up, still soaking wet, and turned the shower off. As he walked me to the bed, he kissed me softly on the lips.

After laying me on my back, he pulled the covers over us and fell between my legs. He pulled me up high because he was so tall. His soft dick rested against my thigh as his head lay on my chest. "Wrap your arms around me, girl. You know I love your touch."

I smiled and wrapped my arms around him, massaging the back of his head. He stuffed his hands under me, grabbing me tighter and pulling me more toward him. He was invasive and so sexy about it. None of my body went cold when he held me. He knew how to make me feel so warm and loved.

Thinking about how he fucked Spin and if he made her feel the same way made me feel somewhat sad. She didn't deserve his intimacy, not like me. I deserved it all.

As he slept peacefully, I smiled. I forgot how good it felt to be under him. Just feeling him breathe and his breath on my body gave me goosebumps.

"I wish you could stay here with me today," I whispered, thinking he was asleep.

"I will, ma."

A gentle kiss was then placed on his forehead, and we both dozed off.

A loud boom woke both of us up from a deep sleep. Instinctively, I reached over and grabbed the gun from under the pillow and tossed it to him. He pulled his briefs over his ass and ran toward the front door, but everything looked fine.

"What was that?" I asked, wiping the sleep from my eyes.

Just as I asked that, we heard Icis screaming for help. Terry snatched the door open to see Icis' door kicked down.

We rushed to her aid, only to find her youngest son, Loc, beating her ass. "What the fuck?!" Terry shoved the gun to me and rushed over to his brother, using his elbow to slam him against the wall into a chokehold. "Are you fucking crazy?!" he yelled at Loc.

Loc's big brown eyes looked so cold in that moment. He stared at Icis like he was about to kill her soon as he was free. His eyes started to turn red, so Terry eased off him a bit and let him speak.

"Get him out my damn house! Out!" Icis cried hysterically.

Her nose was bleeding, and her hair was all over her head. I found a piece of napkin and placed it on her nose. She took it from me and did it herself, holding her head back, so she wouldn't bleed on the floor any more than she'd already done.

"What's wrong with you?" Terry asked his brother.

Loc pointed at his mom, and he too began to cry. "She finally did it. She finally fucked me over, too."

"What she did? Talk to me, lil' bro."

Icis seemed to know she'd fucked up because she started to cower like a guilty dog. "All my work is gone, bro."

"What you mean?"

"Nigga, she broke into my house and cleaned me out. The bitch thought she was slick hiding behind the cameras, not knowing it's hidden ones in the house, too."

Terry shot a mean glare over at Icis. "You stole from Loc? That's why you been out for days? What did you do? Shoot it all up?"

She then pointed at me, leaving me so confused. "It's her fault."

"What?" I asked. "Me?"

"She been stepping on the drugs you told her to give me. Did you know that? She thought I ain't know."

"You know about the morphine?" Terry asked.

"I've been doing this a while. I ain't slow." Soon as she said that, Loc tried to flash out again, but Terry had an army grip on him.

"So, you fuck me over because you ain't happy with the drugs you was given? We agreed to let her step on the shit to get you help, you dumb bitch!" Loc roared. He was hot.

"If you knew about it, then you're just as guilty," she told him. As if she deserved to take his drugs.

"Bitch!" He tried so hard to get away and beat her again, but Terry wouldn't let him. Terry just stood there looking so confused.

"You couldn't have done all his drugs, Mama. What you do with the rest?"

"I don't know. I had done some with a few friends, passed out, and woke up in my doghouse. I think it was stolen." She seemed so unfazed by everything she said.

Loc had just lost so much money, and she treated it like a beach day on vacation.

"I will murder this bitch."

"How much she take?"

"That was thirty thousand dollars worth of work and material. It's all gone. All of it. She even broke my window trying to get in. She dropped some on the floor, and my fucking dog licked it up and died. I hate this hoe! I hate this bitch!" He paced the floor with Terry in his heels to make sure he ain't do nothing crazy. "You got six kids, Icis! Six! And only two still love you. Now you down to one." He tossed a small sonogram photo back in her face. "This is the grandchild you'll never get to fucking see."

It was rumored that he had another baby on the way, but I just wasn't sure. Now I was. The black and white picture of a fetus fell on the table into a cup.

Icis tried to act like seeing Loc leave didn't bother her, but I knew it tore her down on the inside. She loved all her kids. She just had a fucked up way of showing it.

After Loc left, we all stood there in silence. Terry had

forgotten he was out there with nothing but briefs on. Me with only a robe on, it was obvious we'd been having sex. I saw that Icis wanted to comment on it, but she knew now wasn't the time.

"Me and Dad are going to give Loc back what you stole, and after that, you're getting help. Do you understand?"

"I ain't doing shit."

"Yes, you are."

"Shit."

"You will. Know why? All the assistance you had came from me, Loc, and Crystal. Loc is done, and until you do exactly what needs to be done, you will receive no assistance from me."

"You can't make Crystal not help me."

"Her lease is up soon. She won't be right next door anymore. Nobody is going to help. Either you get your shit together, or you're losing everyone, and I mean it." He walked away, brushing past us.

She gave me sad eyes, but I couldn't stay. I had to go and check on him.

Once back in my side of the duplex, I rushed to the bedroom to see him getting dressed. Placing my hand on his shoulder, I said, "Just wait."

"I can't. I gotta handle this today before Loc comes back and does something to her. I need to meet up with my dad, so we can replace what she took, and then I have to hear his mouth about how Loc should've known better than to leave his drugs alone."

"I'll go with you." I knew he didn't need me in the mix, but I just wanted to be there for him. I hated to see him this upset.

"Crystal, move, damn." He tried to pull away but ended up dragging me to the side, making me fall over my nightstand. "Fuck. I didn't mean that, ma. I'm sorry." He helped me up, but my robe slipped off.

Without saying another word, he turned and walked away. "Terry, please! Don't go!" I cried as I bent down to pick my robe back up to put on.

I heard the front door close and lock. "Come here."

He walked back into the room and snatched my robe back off. He pulled his dick from his pants and picked me up, placing my pussy perfectly on his dick. Looking deep into my eyes, he bounced me up and down on his swollen member.

"Terry."

"What's up?" He continued fucking me like I was the one who'd just pissed him off.

"Take your anger out on me. Please," I said.

I knew how he was when he got upset, and I didn't want him to leave the house like that. The last time he was this mad, bodies dropped all over the city. He never was really good at controlling his temper. It took a lot to get him upset, yes, but once he was up, he stayed up there.

He walked over to the bed, still harshly bouncing me on his dick. He then bent me over and grabbed the back of my neck. "Spread them cheeks."

"Okay, daddy." I did as I was told.

He slammed inside of me and fucked me so hard but so good. I didn't notice I was running until I realized he was chasing me onto the bed. "Bring my pussy back to me. Stop running."

I then rested and relaxed. I wanted him to leave there feeling like he's just smoked a fat blunt. "Yes, Daddy! Please, fuck me. Please."

"I can do what I want?"

"Yes, baby."

"I love when you talk like that. Come here."

He pulled my head back, placed his lips over mine, and let his drool fall into my mouth. I loved when he did that. I drank it all and kissed him like I was so hungry for his passion. Shit, I was deeply hungry for his passion. Who was I kidding?

"It's yours, baby."

"It's daddy's?"

"Yes, it's daddy's."

"Cum for daddy then."

On command, I came just like that, and I came super hard. He did, too.

Instead of staying in bed with me like he promised, he pulled his dick back into his pants, grabbed his keys, and left. I felt relieved but hurt at the same time because I knew this didn't mean we were back together.

He was just a toxic ass nigga like that.

Asha
A Rock and A Hard Place

Usually, I would be working on a Saturday, but given the fact that my sister had been with me for two days already, I wanted to spend the weekend making sure she was settled and comfortable.

Sway and Tweety had both come over to check on her and talk to her, making sure her head was on straight. Everything was looking good. Arielle's biggest problem right now was that she was ready for school to start. She also couldn't wait to join theater class and show off her talents in the school musicals. It wasn't set in stone, but I had pretty much made up my mind that Arielle would be with me from this moment on or at least until she was eighteen and ready to leave for college. I would have to rearrange some things, but I would do that for her any time. We had all vowed that she would never go through what we did, and we meant it.

Yes, we still loved Mama Crystal, but if I said life was easy being brought up by her, I would be lying. She made us hard because we had to be.

Arielle was soft, and I wanted her to stay that way. Being hard wasn't necessary. Not to live, it wasn't. Especially if her goal was to leave the streets. I wanted her to stay the sweet little girl she was.

Right now, I was on my way to pick her up from Dennis and Demaris' mom's house. They had a little sister named Bambi. She and Arielle were around the same age and had some of the same classes in school. Ms. Reita let them go swimming in the neighborhood's pool and cooked dinner. Of course, she invited me, and of course, I had to go because I had to pick up Arielle.

I knew it was a bad idea before I even arrived. I just felt it.

Once I got there, Bambi and Arielle ran outside to greet me like the happy teenagers they were. Still with the swim tops on, they both had on booty shorts that were too little for my liking, but I let it go.

"Dennis and Demaris are both here," Arielle whispered to me so Bambi couldn't hear her.

"Good looking out." I gave her a fist pump.

Reita lived in a suburb called Duncanville. It used to be a fantastic side of town, but now it was just mediocre. Everyone from the hood who came across some money went straight there because it was close, and the houses were nicer. Soon, it would be another ghetto.

The house smelled good, like fried chicken, burgers, and links. Reita met us at the door smiling with her lace front slayed to the hair Gods. She was so gorgeous at her current age, so I knew she was something to reckon with when she was my age.

She gave me a big hug. Once she got to my ear, she said, "Meet me in my room in five minutes."

I nodded and embraced her back. I had to act like everything was normal because, apparently, she didn't want anyone to know what she'd said.

Demaris was on the grill, and Dennis was in the kitchen stirring some pork and beans.

The girls ran back to Bambi's room, and I slid upstairs to Reita's room. She closed the door. "I should've told you long ago, but Dennis still has a key to your place, and he's switching out your birth control." She grabbed her chest like this had been sitting heavy on her heart.

I felt so bad for her because I had to act like I ain't know.

"What?"

"Don't be mad at me. I didn't know what to do. As a woman, I know it was wrong to not tell you, but as a mother, I didn't want to go against my son. But, dammit, right is right, and wrong is wrong."

"How long has he been doing this?"

"For a while." Her eyes were full of regret. "He really misses you, Asha. He always tells me how sorry he is about how it all turned out. Just give him another chance."

"After I just found out he's been breaking into my house?" Was she serious?

"It's just that all he talks about is you, and he's not going to stop until you at least give him another chance."

"How long has he been here?" I asked.

I only asked because I wanted to make sure he wasn't trying to talk to my sister while I wasn't around. Demaris said he wouldn't let him, but I wanted to be on the safe side.

"Not long. Actually, he only came about twenty minutes ago when he found out I invited you."

"I'll try to talk to him, but I'm fucked up about the birth control thing and the fact that he still has a key and has been in my home while I'm not there."

I had changed my locks the day after Demaris told me, so I wasn't worried about buddy. He was annoying. To act like I wasn't in love with Demaris would be hard, but if it would keep things peaceful, I was all for it.

We went back down the stairs. It was so hard not to look at Demaris. He looked so good in his fitted black and gold shirt with black jeans. On his feet were some gold Yeezys. He smiled at me, and the light caught his teeth, almost blinding me. I wanted to fuck him right then.

Dennis came up from behind, kissing on me like we were cool. "Glad you came." He held me and gave Demaris the once over.

I pulled away from him. "I came because I was invited by your mother. Arielle was already here."

"Come help us set the table," Arielle said, pulling me away.

"Thank you," I told her.

"That's what sisters are for," she said, and we both laughed.

She'd never liked Dennis much. I couldn't blame her; he was just corny all around. Now that we were over, I couldn't believe I even cried over him. The man did steroids, for crying out loud. If the force knew that, his career would be over. I wanted him to try and flex on me with the situation regarding my family. It wouldn't be smart.

Bambi got a phone call and left the dining room. Demaris came in while it was just Arielle and me setting the table and snuck a feel on my ass.

Arielle winked at us and smiled. "Watch out now," she playfully told him.

"Watch out for what?" Bambi asked, coming back in with a huge smile.

"Watch out for Tree. Ain't he the one who got you blushing like that?" Arielle asked, totally deflecting from what was going on. She always came in the clutch when things got sticky.

"Who the hell is Tree?" Reita asked, coming around the corner with a pan of food.

"Bambi's boo," Arielle snitched.

"Let me see a picture," I said.

She hesitated but pulled out her phone. As I leaned over to look at the picture, Demaris leaned over me. "He looks high as hell," I said.

"That's why they call him Tree. He's cute, right?" she asked, looking nervous.

"He i'ght," Reita and I said in unison.

"Man, I'll shoot that nigga," Demaris said, putting some space between us.

"He cute, he cute," Arielle said, tapping Bambi's shoulder.

"See, you always got my back, Arielle," she joked.

"You need to be in them books and not worried about no nappy head niggas anyway," Dennis scolded as he came around the corner.

She rolled her eyes. "Here you go."

"And y'all sitting here feeding into that shit," Dennis said, placing more food on the table.

"They're just being kids. Relax," Reita told him as she tapped his shoulder and shook her head.

"It's the summer anyway. Let them be young ladies," I added as I sat down.

"I just don't want my little sister turning out like these other girls around the city, gang banging, popping pussy, and killing. Need I say more?" He sat across from me.

"Dennis, please hush," Bambi said as she and Arielle also sat down.

I wanted to relax, but I couldn't because Dennis was staring at me like he didn't know if he wanted to punch me or kiss me. This was really getting old.

For a few minutes, we were all quiet as we filled our plates until Dennis broke the silence. His lame behind went straight for the kill.

"So, Arielle, what happened when you called the police the other day?"

I dropped my fork. "Dennis."

Without looking at me, he said, "I'm just a concerned police officer who was asked to leave the scene. I just want to make sure I didn't leave a minor in a compromised situation."

Reita shook her head and gave him a mean stare. One so mean that I wasn't sure what she would do next. "Dennis, you need to change the subject."

Arielle kept a smile on her face, but I could tell she was humiliated.

That sent me over the edge. "You would put my sister's feelings in jeopardy to get under my skin? Are you that pathetic?" I asked before I knew it.

He ignored me and steadily interrogated my sister. "Arielle, if you're in danger, you know you can come to me."

"I'm staying with Asha now."

"Oh, okay. Yeah. That's great. So, did you guys take it through the courts and do this thing legally? Or are you a runaway?"

"Dennis, you need to chill, my nigga," Demaris said, sliding his plate away.

I couldn't fucking believe Dennis right now. He was out of his rabbit mind to think this was any kind of way to get me back.

"Because if you're a runaway, I need to report it." He looked over at me and winked. "Ain't that right, suga?"

I took the glass of water from in front of me and tossed it on him. My hands were shaking. Everyone at the table was silent.

For a second, it got really still until Dennis hopped to his feet and attempted to reach me over the table, but Demaris grabbed his hand and pushed him back into the chair.

Reita stood up and slammed her fist on the table. "Dennis, dammit, you get'cho ass upstairs right now." She stormed past him.

When she saw he didn't move, she circled back and pulled him by the ear like he was a small child.

"Ouch, Mama! Damn! Okay!" He yanked away from her and followed her up the stairs. "You okay?" I asked Arielle.

She nodded, but her face was red. "Yes. Of course. Everything is fine."

I reached over and grabbed her hand. "If you want to leave, we can."

"Oh, no. This is fine. It's just a love tap, and I got caught in the middle. He's just emotional about your cold shoulder. I get it."

"He doesn't have to be a bitch about it," Bambi said, looking at the stairs in disgust.

"He tried to hit me," I said.

"He wasn't gon' fuck with you," Demaris assured me.

Bambi wiped the water from the table for me. I was still shaking and didn't trust myself to walk or make big movements.

As I sat at the table, I wondered what I was waiting for. I didn't want to be there any longer and didn't owe anyone an explanation, so I decided it was time for Arielle and me to go. She wasn't upset about it either. We said our goodbyes, but Reita was still yelling at Dennis upstairs.

We quickly made our way to the car. On the way home, we stopped and got some burgers since we really didn't eat at the table.

"He knows he tried it," Arielle said as we walked into my apartment.

"Fuck him. He don't have shit else to say to me. If he wants to take it there, we can take it there. I don't have nothing for a coward."

"I heard that. I'm about to play the game," she said as she kissed my cheek and walked away to the guest bedroom, which was hers now, I guess.

Once in my room, I checked my phone to see that I had many missed calls from Dennis and a text from Demaris asking if I was okay. I texted Demaris back and told him we were fine, just at home relaxing. I texted Dennis and told him to lose my number.

The more I thought about it, the more I felt like Dennis was upset because I hadn't let him have sex with me. I truly believed he was desperately trying to trap me with a child by him.

After getting comfortable, I lay in bed and positioned myself exactly where the moon was shining down on me. While it was on my mind a little bit, I called Tweety to make sure Mama Crystal had been checked into rehab. "Yo?" she answered.

"You want to be a nigga so bad. How it go today?"

"The rehab for Ma?"

"Duh," I said. "What else was I talking about? You damn sure ain't going to rehab."

"Oh, it went good. She actually didn't put up any fight."

"Did Sway take her at gunpoint?" I asked in a joking way.

"Actually, she did. She had to pull a gun to get her into the car. Also, she told her if she fucks this up, she will kill her before the disease does to put her out of her misery."

"Crazy thing is, I believe her."

"Oh, after this, she ain't playing with Ma no more. Should've seen the fear in Ma's eyes. She knows she fucked up this time."

"What about the house?"

"What about it?" she wanted to know.

"Is it cleaned? The last time I saw it, it was a mess."

"Oh, yeah, I paid Rel and a few of her friends to slide through and clean it. Since her ass can't be good for nothing else."

"I think Rel gon' be a problem in the future. That's been on my mind tough."

"You sound like all rest of us. We just don't know what to do about her. That's why I've been keeping her busy with miscellaneous shit, so she can still feel included. I don't know."

"Maybe we should give her back to her community. She ain't thriving over here."

"Yeah, and then what? She tells all of our business? I'm sure we can find some use for her."

"We'll see. I ain't heard about her being no witness, so that's good."

I heard Tweety snap her fingers like she'd just remembered something. "While it's fresh on my mind, tell me why I been hearing that Ski Man been running his mouth."

"That was expected."

"Nah," she said like there was more. "This boy is mad *mad*. He's making some crazy threats."

I sat up in bed at full attention. "Like what?" I asked, thinking about what Delyle had told me.

"I don't know how true it is, but everyone is saying it. Supposedly, he's saying he's going to kidnap Arielle."

"Girl, if he had that in play, he wouldn't tell the streets about it. He's bluffing. Bitch just mad I pistol whipped him in front of his minions."

"That's something crazy to say, though, you know?"

"Why do you sound scared?"

"I'm not. I'm worried."

"Why are you worried?"

"Why you not worried?"

"Because we grew up with him, Tweety. You know just as well as me how he be talking shit. He's a bitch. Everyone knows that."

"For the next few weeks, we're just going to keep an extra eye on Arielle. If he does anything to her, if he even looks at her, I'm torturing that boy. I promise."

"You and me both."

She sighed. "Asha?"

I knew that sigh anywhere. She had something on her mind. And whatever it was, it had been on her mind. "Yes."

"Never mind."

"Tell me."

"It's nothing."

"You sure?"

"I am. Get some rest. I love you." She hung up.

I wanted to call back, but I was too exhausted.

SPIN
TIME FOR INVESTIGATION

I had finally gotten the drop on where Terry's ex lived, and the way I went about it, I wasn't proud.

After she popped up at his apartment that morning with the dog, I knew she had to live close by.

One morning, Terry had to settle a dispute between his brother and mother, and since it took up most of his day, I took it upon myself to let Diamond out a few streets over and follow her to her next destination.

We ended up at a duplex over by the border between Arlington and Ft Worth. She sniffed around this duplex for about an hour, so I jotted the address down and took Diamond home.

I came back around the time I knew the bitch said she got off and waited. Sure enough, this duplex belonged to her.

From what I had seen, her mornings consisted of checking the home next to hers and then going home. I wondered what was so special about her that she was close to him and his personal life. I mean, the dog even ran away to her house. I had to know what was going on and if he was still messing around with her.

The streets were still fairly quiet at that time of the morning until a loud, single bang came on my passenger window. "Hey!"

A woman was looking into my car with bucked eyes. The

most beautiful but disturbing eyes. Her hair looked to be of a good grade but was slightly matted. Her skin tone was hidden under ash and dead skin, but it was still clearly beautiful.

I checked my jeep for a couple of dollars and slid the window down just enough to throw it at her. "Here, now get away from my whip." I tossed the money and rolled the window back up.

Today wasn't the day for a junkie to harass me for money. It was too much going on, and my man, who wasn't supposed to be my man, was possibly cheating on me. If she made a scene, I would be caught out there stalking little miss Crystal, and I wasn't having that.

"I know you," she said. "I've seen your pictures."

Junkies always swore up and down they knew someone. "Look, lady, I gave you the money. Move." I flashed my gun at her to show her I meant business.

She giggled at me like I was a complete joke. "That's cute," she said, still staring at me. She hadn't blinked, not once. Not that I'd noticed. She was odd, to say the least. "Looks like the gun my son pistol whipped me with the other day."

"Bye, lady." I rolled my eyes.

She started banging on my window, with each bang being more aggressive than the previous one. "Get away from here! I know what you're doing! You have no business here!"

"Go the fuck away. Last time asking."

She continued to bang on my window, so I drove down the street and circled the block. I thought I had lost her until she came out of nowhere and slowly walked in front of my car like a zombie, only with her head turned my way. "What the fuck?" I asked myself. This lady was on a new kind of drug. I wanted the name of it so I could sell it.

"You won't win," she said loudly.

"Win what?"

"His heart."

I blew her off, trying to back up, but I had parked in front of a car. The only way I could get out was forward, and this bitch wouldn't move. "You don't know me, and I don't know you. Just move, and I'll leave. You doing too much."

Suddenly, like a grasshopper, she hopped on the hood of my jeep and started kicking at my window.

I had no remorse at this point, junkie or not. I had warned her. "Fuck it." I mashed the gas and sped to the stop sign with her holding on.

She looked me dead in the eyes and still didn't seem not one bit bothered. I mashed the gas, sending her flying several feet away onto the main road.

It all happened so fast. She lay there, laughing like a maniac and pointing at me. I got out of the jeep and tried to help her up, but a car flying by beat me to it.

I turned my head, so I couldn't see it. I only heard it. Some of her blood even splashed onto my fingernails. My shoulders stiffened as I held in a loud scream.

The car didn't even turn around. The Hyundai had even run the light.

I wanted to stay and help, but I knew that wouldn't be smart. She lay there looking like a distorted stick figure.

After rushing back to my car, I tore up the dash console to find the spare burner phone that I kept for emergencies. Frantically, I called the cops and gave them the intersection of the body.

Before driving off, I got back out to move her body out of the middle of the street. It was still a bit dark, and I didn't want anyone to run the frail body over even more. I heard her bones crack as I dragged her into a yard nearby.

As I was about to run away, I heard soft noises coming from behind me.

"Don't leave," she said just above a whisper.

I almost turned and went back, but I had to keep going. I just prayed to God that she understood if she made it.

TERRY
THEY CALL IT SOUL TIES

We'd been at the hospital all day. Early this morning, I'd gotten a call from Crystal saying that a coworker of hers told her about Icis being rushed to the hospital. My mom had been hit by a car and left for dead. She'd just gotten out of surgery, and her chances of making it were slim to none—this was what the doctor personally told me.

I paced around the waiting room, not really sure of what to do. My mom wasn't the best mom, but all I could think about was the mom she was before the drugs and heartache. All I could visualize was her pretty smile. It was crazy how tragedy rearranged things.

Spin sat by the vending machines, and Crystal stood over by the nurses' station, getting all the information she could.

"I never even got to meet her," Spin said with water welling in her eyes.

She'd been more upset than me. For someone who had never met Icis a day in her life, she had a heavy heart about it. That made me feel even worse about the role I played in her brother's death. There she was, crying over my family drama with the man who killed her brother. I wanted to just break the news right now with so much tragedy floating around, but I declined to do so. That would only make matters worse.

"All hope isn't lost, love. You still could meet her."

Who was I kidding? Crystal was informed that my mom had bones broken all over her body, and it was almost impossible for her brain to function again. The only thing keeping her alive was the machine.

Loc was crying into his palms as his baby mama rubbed his back. His long, Bone Thug and Harmony braids hung over his face. "It's okay, baby. I'm here," she said.

"No, it's not, bro. I pistol whipped my mama over some drugs, man." He looked at her with such a sadness that I had never seen on him before. "Fuck them drugs. I got that shit back the same day. Dad replaced it all. But Mama? She can't be replaced." He stood to his feet and dragged his way to the men's restroom.

His baby mama looked at me like she didn't know what to do and wanted me to step in. "I got it," I said as I went into the restroom and locked the door.

He was standing in front of the mirror, looking at himself quite the same way I stared at myself when I was at Mama's house the other day.

"It's spooky looking at yourself. Isn't it?" I asked, standing next to him. Our resemblance was undeniable. He was just darker with long hair.

"I'm fucked up, my nigga." Both hands were on the countertop. He could barely hold himself up.

"You ain't gotta be. I'm here for you 'til the wheels fall off."

He shook his head. "I pistol whipped my mama, cuzz." He started pulling on his braids and backed into the stalls. "I pistol whipped my fucking mama, my nigga."

I snatched him over to me and pulled him in for a tight embrace. "We all make mistakes. All of us."

His tears were wetting my shirt. "But we don't make mistakes like this. Who the fuck pistol whips they own mama? She ain't even deserve all that. It wasn't even that deep. That shit was lame, bro." He was hyperventilating.

I had never in life seen him like this. Not Loc. He was up there with our dad when it came to not caring about shit that crossed us.

"You weren't thinking."

"What if she jumped in front of that car? What if what I did and said pushed her to jump? Have we even considered that possibility?"

"Mama ain't did no shit like that. Someone ran her over and left."

"She fucked Junior over bad, and he ain't ever put his hands on her. She did the same shit to Malory, Christian, you, and Franco, and neither of y'all ever put y'all hands on her. I tripped out." He was right. She'd messed over all her kids at some point, and we never hit her. They would just leave her alone. "How long until they get here?" he asked.

"Junior is on the way from the airport now, and he got Franco with him. Christian and Malory are on the way. They should be here before dark."

"They bringing all them kids?" he asked.

I felt where he was coming from. Mama was on her death bed, and I didn't have the patience to deal with all the kids they had collectively. It was going to be too much.

"Nah, Dad told them to leave the kids for this trip."

He nodded. "That's good. I ain't want to say nothing, but the last thing I needed was to be surrounded by all them bad ass kids."

I laughed. "I'm already knowing."

"I see Crystal out there."

"Yeah, she was here before all of us."

"You know you did her wrong, though."

"She ain't sad no more. Trust me." I smirked.

He wiped the tears from his eyes and grinned. "You ain't put the *I'm sorry* dick on her. Nah, I know you ain't do no shit like that."

"I did."

"That's why she in the same room with you and that psycho bitch of yours. She ready to risk it all."

"Chill, nigga." I laughed. "Spin cool. She more fucked up about this than I am."

"Fuck she sad about? She ain't even know Icis."

I pushed his shoulder. "She knows *me*, nigga."

"I feel you. She seems like she likes to fight a lot."

"She got a nasty attitude. Nothing that can't be fixed with this Mr. Hammer. Fuck you mean?"

As we continued making jokes, there was a knock. I unlocked it. It was Crystal. "He's here," is all she said. We already knew she meant Delyle.

Loc and I fixed ourselves up and exited the restroom. "He's in the room she's being held in," she told me.

"I thought they said we couldn't go back?" Loc said.

That's when I remembered that Dad's wife was a well-respected doctor in the Dallas-Ft Worth metroplex. Though she did a lot of plastic surgeries, she still was a great doctor all around and had saved many lives. She was a high-ranking doctor, not only at this hospital but at several others. I was sure she got him access to Icis.

Crystal told us how to get to the room. We followed directions, getting lost several times before actually finding the room.

Dad stood over her with his hand on top of her broken hand. Though he didn't cry, he was visibly torn apart. One would have to know him to see how hurt he was. His hand being on hers was a top indicator that he was sad. He never did that, especially not to Icis. He hadn't talked to her in years, let alone touched her.

"She's not going to make it," he said in a monotone.

"We know," I said.

Loc stepped back and tried to hide the fact that he was crying.

"It's okay, Lionel," Dad said to him. He hated the nickname the streets gave Loc, so he never used it. Dad was the only person in the world who was allowed to call Loc his birth name, Lionel.

He really didn't have a choice. He couldn't tell dad not to call him Lionel, and he knew that. He never even tried to do such a thing.

"My bad," Loc said, trying to toughen up.

"No need to apologize. Her nose is broken. Was that the car, or did that come from your incident with her?"

Loc was shaken to the core. He didn't want to answer that because he knew the answer would be upsetting.

Dad turned his head back, looking down at the floor. Loc stood feet away from him. "I asked you a question."

"Me."

"What did you hit your mom with for her nose to break?" he asked. We never told him he pistol whipped Mama before I could stop him. That part we left out. "Lionel!" he roared.

"My gun."

"You hit your mom, a woman, with a gun? Is that what you're telling me?"

"Yes, sir."

Dad turned back to face Mama. The tubes coming from her mouth, the bandages, the twisted frame, it all was sad to look at. Dad removed his gun from the small of his back and checked the safety. Loc didn't look frightened. He knew Dad would never shoot him.

He turned to Loc and smashed the butt of the gun against his head three times until Loc fell onto the couch.

Mom's machine started beeping. Her heart rate went up, stopping Dad from hitting Loc again. Even on her deathbed, she protected her children.

Dad used a Kleenex and hand sanitizer to clean the blood from his hand. He then tossed the box of Kleenex down to Loc. "Clean yourself up. Now."

Loc snatched the Kleenex from the box and held it against his nose just like Mom did when he made hers bleed. "She stole from m—"

He attempted to explain, but Dad put his hand up,

prohibiting him from speaking. He slammed down onto the couch and nursed his bleeding nose.

"Everything okay?" Crystal asked. "The machines alerted the nurses. I told them I would get it." She briefly saw a suffering Loc and quickly removed her attention from him and put it back on Dad and me.

"It's fine. My wife is here. Can you please bring her to me?" he said.

"Yes, sir." She walked away.

"I don't give a damn what she did. Hitting her was enough, but pistol whipping your mother? Are you crazy?" He was finally ready to resume.

"You're the one who taught us not to let nobody play with us. Nobody."

"She's your mother! You never disrespect your parents. You treat her how you treat me."

"You would never steal from me."

He had a point, but he was still wrong. I understood both sides, nevertheless. "That's brutal force against a woman who didn't put your life in danger."

"What if I ain't have you? Huh? What if a nigga had fronted me them drugs, and her actions got me killed?"

"That's not *your* reality. Your reality is that you have a mother who's a junkie and a father that's been reimbursing his children for her fuckups for years. She was no threat whatsoever. That's your reality."

"So what? You was gon' keep reimbursing us forever?"

"You don't understand how valuable life is. You do now, but you never did. She's dead, and your last memory of her is beating her and breaking her nose. That's going to be your karma. That's going to be what you have to live with for the rest of your life. Are you ready?"

Loc took a minute to respond. He was crying and trying to stop the bleeding from his nose. "I don't think I am."

"Well, you have no choice."

"Yes, baby?" Veronica's sweet voice echoed from across the room.

"Lionel's nose might be broken. What can we do?"

She walked over to Loc and sat next to him. "Put your head back." She grabbed the Kleenex and looked into his nose. "It's not broken. Just busted it a bit. Who did this to you?" He didn't answer, but the vibes told her it was our dad. "Come with me. I'll get you all fixed up."

They left, and Crystal walked back inside. "How long does she have?" Dad asked her. She sighed like she was about to beat around the bush, but he quickly cut her off. "Don't bullshit me. Give it to me straight."

"Without the machine, she won't make it past an hour. But her organs are already crashing, so I say about two weeks, maybe less."

He nodded. "Thanks."

"Can I talk to you?" she asked.

"Yeah."

I let her lead the way to the hall. All her nosey ass friends tried to act like they weren't paying attention, but they were. She peeped, too, so she pulled me into the bathroom and locked the door.

"I haven't heard from you."

"I'm not about to do this with you right now."

She crossed her arms over her chest and exhaled. Her eyes looked deep into mine. It was like she pulled out every emotion I had in me with just one look. "What?" she asked, noticing my uneasy look.

"How do you do that?"

"Do what?"

"Make me feel you without being inside of you," I said. It was true. I felt all her feelings and mine. I couldn't explain.

"I think they call it soul ties." She took her soft hand and placed it on my cheekbone.

"I think that's what it is."

"Will I hear from you later on today? Or at all this week?"

"I don't know."

"Is it because of today's events or because of the girl waiting for you in the family room?"

"Both."

She bit her top lip. "What we did the other day means nothing to you."

"We had sex, Crystal. We've had sex many times."

"How do you fuck someone like that and don't think about them again?"

"I do think about you."

"Yeah? When I think about people, I call them. I reach out to them in some way."

I turned my head. "What do you want from me?"

"I want you to tell me what I need to do for us to work things out. Who do I need to be? Tell me."

"This was a fear of mine," I said.

"What?"

"You trying to be someone else just for me." I leaned over and kissed her in the mouth. "I'll call you when I can." I left her in the bathroom.

Once in the room with Dad, he said, "I saw you have them both here."

"Crystal was here before me. Spin was already at my house, so she rode with me up here."

"They gave you any problems?"

"Nope. Crazy, huh?"

"Not really."

"If Mama pulls through with some miracle happening, will you ever speak to her again?"

"No," he answered immediately.

"One day, will you ever tell me what she did that was so wrong?"

"We have six children, but we're supposed to have eight."

"Two more?"

He nodded, still looking down at Mama. "She aborted them. First, she lied to me and told me it was a miscarriage, but I found the papers confirming the completion of an abortion."

I never knew that, and I would've never guessed it. "Why would she do that?"

"I don't think they were mine."

"Are all of us yours?"

"Yes. After that, I tested all six of you, and you all are mine. Those twins belonged to someone else. I'm almost one hundred percent sure."

"Damn. I ain't even know all this."

He backed away from the bed and stared out the window. "I want a one hundred thousand dollar bounty on whoever did this. I want them brought to me alive. Put the word out."

SPIN
HEAVILY OFFENDED

"Can you at least talk to me?"

It was three in the morning, and Terry had been keeping his distance. The hospital had pretty much told us that his mother was badly injured and wasn't going to make it. That struck me hard because this was all my fault. My conscience was ripping me apart on the inside.

"Listen, you ain't been home in a few days. I know your people will start to worry soon." He was counting up money, seemingly in his tunnel vision.

"I want to be here for you. Damn. Let me just be your girl."

"You ain't doing shit but annoying me, bro. This ain't even the time for all that."

"Fuck it." I plopped down on the bed and watched him handle his business. He had shown little to no interest in me since the news broke about his mom.

To find out that it was his mom I helped kill cut me deep. Now that I thought back, she looked identical to Loc. Then she was in front of Crystal's duplex. Why didn't I make that connection? All of this could've been avoided if I had just left the moment she made me out. That was the smart thing to do. Now she was lying on her death bed, and an entire family would be torn apart.

"Hey, I know this is crazy to ask, but one night, me and the girls went out to the club of the man who kidnapped Sway. I was a little tipsy that night, but the man looked identical to the man I just saw at the hospital yesterday. I guess what I'm asking is—"

"Yes. Delyle is my father."

One had to be in my shoes to understand how drained I was with this week. It was something every single day. "That's how you were so sure he wouldn't hurt her when he had her. Right?"

"Yeah, man. So what?" He slapped a rubber band on some money and tossed it onto the TV stand.

"You didn't feel the need to tell me?"

"Why I need to tell you who my father is?"

"Because he had my fucking friend in a basement. That's why."

"And that same friend has made a friend out of my father. She seems to not be tripping, so why are you?"

"You sat in my face and watched me stress over Sway, knowing your fucking father had her. You don't think that's wrong?" I was halfway off the bed, ready to slap him in his face.

"Fuck that bitch."

"What?"

"Even so, I knew he wasn't going to hurt her."

"How did you know?"

"Because if he wanted her dead, he would have been done it."

"You don't know that, stupid ass nigga!" I was now off the bed and on my feet. I muffed him so hard that it caused a natural reflex. He dropped the money, grabbed my arm, and forced it behind my back. He used his feet to trip me to the ground and held me down. "Get off me! I can't breathe!" The pressure from his elbow was hurting me like hell.

He finally freed me, then snatched his tank top off and pointed at the door. "Get out."

Grabbing my neck, I said, "What?"

"Get out my sight. I don't want to see you. I don't want to be around you. Just leave. You stressing me out."

"All I did was ask a —"

"Get out, bro, damn. What, I got to physically kick you out? Burn out."

Without another word, I grabbed my small bag, shoes, and keys. I knew I was doing too much, but I was in too deep to try and apologize. Emotions were already too high. Honestly, I had no reason to be upset. It just felt better to have something to be mad about because of how I had just possibly changed his life for the worse.

While sitting in the jeep, I lit a cigarette. For one, I didn't even know I had cigarettes. Two, I had only smoked one twice before, and that's when I was stressed beyond belief. This was one of those times.

Terry and I being somewhat of a secret was getting to me because I badly wanted to vent to Sway. She would have a solution. Shaking my head and looking up at his apartment, I called Asha instead. She also had solutions for problems. Calling her was maybe for the best anyway because her solutions didn't involve anyone getting hurt most of the time.

"Everything okay?" Asha asked.

"Yeah but no. It's not a dire problem, though."

"You sound disturbed. What is it then?"

"I ran over Terry's mom before I knew it was his mom." I took a deep breath. "Think I may have killed her."

"Is this a joke?"

"I wish it was."

"What the fuck, Spin? How? How did you even allow this?"

I ran her through it all, detail by detail. Every single thing. "You think anyone saw me?"

"If you weren't by any stop lights, there's a great chance you got away."

"Thank God."

"His mother? This is by far one of the most insensitive things you've done."

Resting my elbow on the window, I said, "I think if I tell him what happened and how it happened, then maybe he'll understand. What do you think?" I exhaled the nasty smoke.

"I couldn't have heard you right. Don't make me clock out and come slap you. Are you crazy?"

I thought about it for a second and quickly realized I was tripping. "You're right. Then, I didn't know his dad was the same guy who took Sway." Instead of looking at it as I had just killed my man's mother, I started to look at it as I had just killed Delyle's baby mother. Suddenly, shit got a little more complicated for me. "In my defense, she hopped on my car. What was I supposed to do? Tell me."

"You're starting to sound like Sway. You didn't have to throw her off the car into oncoming traffic. That was a bit much, and you know it." She was right. "It wasn't her that pissed you off that morning. You were already mad about the fact of you watching Crystal."

Speaking of Crystal, I saw her creeping up the stairs and onto my man's floor. At first, I thought I was tripping until I saw her actually take a deep breath, then walk in front of his door and knock. "Let me call you back." I tossed the cigarette and hung up before she even had a chance to protest.

Before getting out of the car, I slid my shoes off because I already knew I would have to take it there. This was not how I imagined today going.

Once my hand touched the railing, I skipped up the stairs, taking two at a time. When I finally landed in front of his door, he noticed me before she did. "I can't stop thinking about you. Baby, you can't stand there and honestly tell me that I don't cross your mind." Her soft voice and the fact that she was wiping her face let me know she was in tears.

"Why are you here, once again, when you're not supposed to be?" I walked over to stand between her and Terry, but he pulled me behind him, making sure to keep the distance between her and me.

Without even acknowledging me, she kept her eyes on him, pleading for his love. "You touch me the way you do and expect me to just leave well enough alone."

"Touch? Like in present tense?" I jerked my head to Terry. "When did you touch her?"

"Don't do this, Crystal." He placed his back against the wall and massaged his temple.

"Do what? I came here not to start drama but for my own peace of mind. I want you to tell me why."

"Why what?" he barked, causing me and her to flinch. The veins in his neck were poking.

"Why do you hurt me the way you do? What have I ever done besides love you? I try my best to be what you need from me. You won't let me."

"Because you do shit like this."

"Excuse me?" I asked him. "No, you diss her because you have a woman. It has everything to do with me."

"You can't tell me how I feel, my nigga," he said with annoyance in his voice.

I shook my head and tossed my hands up. "Okay, so what the fuck is going on?" I was lost.

"Fuck this shit." He brushed past me and slid his shoes on.

"Where you going?" she asked.

"Where the fuck you going?" I wanted to know also. Trying to stand in front of him and block him from leaving, I was pushed to the side. "Bitch," I snapped, trying to swing at him and hit him in the face, but he caught my hand and then grabbed me by the neck, slamming me against the wall.

"You want me to show you that side of me you keep hearing about? Hmm?" His lips were pressed together with the look of Satan in his eyes. "I will beat the shit out of you to the point of brain damage and go on about my day. Touch me again." He dared me.

Once he jerked back, I could finally breathe again. My hands slapped against my knees as I kneeled over to puke.

Crystal hurriedly jumped out of his walking path so she wouldn't even touch him by accident. She seemed to have known something more sinister about him than I did. He hadn't choked her, but for some reason, she was the one walking around with the fear of God.

Once he made it down the stairs, he took off down the street —just walking with his hands behind his head.

"Baby!" I ran behind him, and so did she. We almost tripped over each other, trying to rush down the stairs. "Move, bitch! What the fuck are you even doing?" I asked as I made sure to keep a few feet ahead of her.

"Terry, come back," she said once we both hit the street.

"Bro, y'all bitches gone on somewhere." He shook his head. "Damn, man." He picked up the phone. "Ay, Loc, come get me, my nigga. I'm about to share my location."

When he said that, Crystal stopped and turned back around. I should've done the same thing, but like a dumb ass, I kept walking until we got to the stop sign.

"Can we go back inside?" I asked, standing behind him, being careful not to touch him again.

"Go home, Spin."

"Why?"

"My nigga, I'm about to lose my mama, and you out here trying to fight on me and start shit. Gone on before I spazz out."

"Baby, I'm sorry. Just please come inside, so we can talk."

Instead of responding, he stood in silence. It was dark, so I couldn't tell if he was breathing hard or hyperventilating. All I knew was I wasn't trying to get choked again.

Loc must have lived close because, within ten minutes of Terry calling him, he swerved onto the pavement, almost hitting me in the process.

This was my last chance to try and get Terry to stay. As he

opened the car door, I grabbed his hand. He jerked around and muffed me so hard that I flew into the stop sign.

Loc hopped out of the car and rushed over to me with his hand on the gun in his pants. He almost made it to me until Terry stood in front of him. "You tripping. That's a female."

"Tell that bitch to stay away from my car. I already don't like that hoe." He walked away from me and back to the car. He still had bandages around his nose. I knew he didn't have the bandages when he got to the hospital, but he did by the time we left.

"Go home, Spin. On some real shit. You doing way too much out here."

"Are you going to call me?" I asked, standing to my feet.

"Just chill, damn." He slammed the door, and they were gone.

I should've just walked away like Crystal did. He and his brother were complete lunatics. The fact that Loc showed me his gun heavily offended me. I wouldn't let it slide.

Sway
The Golden Call

I was leaving the trap in south Dallas when I received the golden call.

It had been two long weeks since I had heard from Delyle. To see his number pop up on my phone put a tingle right on my clit.

"Yes?"

"Where are you?" he asked, sounding like he was all alone.

"Leaving one of the traps. What's up?"

"Come to me."

"Where?" I asked almost immediately.

He slightly laughed at my ambition. "Home."

Oh, wow. He invited me to the house this time and not the club. That was a huge step for us, considering he'd put me out the last time we'd seen each other.

"Now?"

"Yes." He hung up.

I was already on the highway, so I turned around and went in the opposite direction toward where he was.

It took about forty minutes, but when I pulled up, he was waiting for me. He sat on the porch with a blunt in his hand. The light shined on him, so his pajama pants and no shirt looked gorgeous from where I was. He seemed to have something on his mind. Though I didn't know him well, I was sure something had him on edge.

I locked the door and walked over to the porch. Just as I was about to sit and join him, he stood and led me inside. "Feels nice to actually be invited back under different circumstances."

He closed the door behind us and led me to a familiar place—the basement. The only lights on were some red led lights and blue lights coming under the bed that wasn't there last time I was there. It made the room dim, sexy and relaxing

"It's a new tone."

"I'm sure." He rubbed my arms from behind, sending a chill down my spine. "Get onto the bed and remove all your clothing."

"Okay." I did as he said with a quickness but still kept some sexiness about myself. Didn't want to seem too eager to please, or maybe that's what he wanted.

Standing in front of me, he stepped out of his expensive house slides and sat in the chair facing me. "Lay on your back and spread your legs."

"Which way?"

"I want your pussy facing me. Open your legs and place two fingers on your clit."

"Okay."

"I love how you're responding, letting me know you understand. Good girl. Massage your clit."

I did it.

"No, more gentle than that."

"Okay." I moaned as I felt his wet finger slide into me.

"How does it feel?"

"Good. Umm."

"Do you like this?" He also slid his thumb into my ass with two fingers now in my pussy. That added to me playing with my clit, and those lights put me in a deep meditation vibe.

"I love it."

"Good girl. You want to cum for daddy?"

He must've felt my pelvis loosen and legs lock. I nodded and bit down on my bottom lip.

"Say it."

"I want to cum for daddy."

"Why do you want to cum for daddy?"

"I want to please you."

"Good girl," he said as I came hard. He used a little more aggression as I came and then went softer once I reached the climax.

"I want you," I said, still feeling the pressure from my orgasm.

"What you want from me?"

"You." Without a verbal response, he leaned back and relaxed the chair, staring at my face over my wide spread legs. "Am I allowed to ask questions?"

"You are."

"What's on your mind?"

"It's nothing I can't handle."

"But it's still something."

"I knew a woman like you before."

This caught my attention, so I positioned myself on my stomach, facing him, with my chin rested on my hands.

"Yeah? When?"

"Before I became who I am, she got the last part."

"Yeah?" I wanted him to go deeper.

"I had come here briefly with my parents. We were fresh from Jamaica, and I was the only one in the house who spoke English. I only planned to finish school here and move on, but she had other plans."

"Who? Your mom?"

"No, the girl I knew like you. She was everything my parents and I didn't want for me. She was wild." He paused and looked up at the wall, seemingly becoming lost. "She went against everything I stood for. Every boundary, every wall I had built, she tore through them so effortlessly. I often trouble myself thinking maybe it's because I was so young." His eyes then found my eyes again. "I still left after finishing school, and my family moved to another state, but it didn't stop her and me. I kept finding my way back here."

"I know you were in love with her but was she in love?"

"Yes, she was. Ironic thing is, she knew she loved me when she met me. I knew I loved her when I lost her."

"What happened to her?"

He looked as if he wanted to answer but went back to the topic instead. "She was a weakness of mine, and I knew that early on. If I hadn't left her, I would've killed her."

I tried not to let my facial expression show how afraid I was. So many thoughts when through my head, but only one stayed. "What made you think of her?"

"I saw her recently." He stood and walked over to the nightstand. When his hand appeared, there was a magnum in it. "I'm nothing like you think I am," he said, sliding the condom on his dick. "Bend over."

I did as I was told.

His warm and heavy dick slid into me with ease but met some resistance as it tried to get in some more. I winced and moaned as I relaxed and allowed him deeper into me. "Be easy, please," I found myself asking.

"Do you want me to stop?" He kept stroking.

I grabbed his hand and shook my head no.

He got more into the bed, and with every move, the deeper he went. He felt so good I could've screamed.

With his thumbs, he pressed into my back, forcing an arch. As he pounded me, all I could think about was what he said about the woman I reminded him of and the detail behind why he left her, even though I was feeling lovely. There was fear mixed with ecstasy.

He made my body feel like I was in heaven, and it shocked me. Not because I didn't expect him to, but because I thought he would do more damage. He confused me with his gentle touch. Maybe he wasn't who I thought he was.

At that point, I ain't know who I thought he was. I just knew he was powerful and well calculated with a built-in aphrodisiac.

After he was sure I had cum, he plopped his large member out of me, leaving me to feel relieved.

"Clean yourself up." He tossed me a towel.

Doing as I was told, I turned to see him watching me as I cleaned myself. "Everything okay?"

"You learn fast."

"Two weeks was enough time to learn."

He smirked. "I see you made good use of your time."

"Now I know what not to do."

"I'm not talking about you and me."

"Then what?"

"The streets talk. I like what I'm hearing about the way you've been handling controversy."

I wanted to ask him if his son was the one telling him how I'd been conducting myself in the streets, but I remembered what happened the last time I mentioned his son.

He walked me back to the car and sent me off. He wasn't his usual self. I didn't know his usual self, but he wasn't the way he usually was with me. I probably would never know what was wrong with him.

When I got back home, I was surprised to see Spin on the couch watching TV. She'd been gone lately, and if she was home, she wasn't for long. Not to mention her attitude had been shitty.

"What are you watching?" I asked as I poured myself a shot of Hennessy. After taking my shot rather quickly, I decided to put some in a cup and share it with her.

"I think I may have killed someone," she said as I plopped next to her on the couch. She was watching old '90s sitcoms, something she hated, so I knew she was serious about what she'd just said.

I passed my cup to her. "So, why do you look like you just killed someone?" Spin never was the type to sulk about a body.

She finished most of the drink. Yeah, she was dead serious. "I didn't mean to this time."

"Who was it."

She glanced over at me and back at the TV. "I don't know."

Wow. For the first time since we were kids, Spin had just lied to me. She never *not* knew who it was that she drilled on. It took me by complete surprise. I didn't want to make a huge deal out of it because she seemed pretty distant and distraught. Whereas I felt the total opposite being that I'd just gotten some of the best dick I'd ever had. For a moment, I almost drifted into bliss, and then I remembered the remark she made.

"Maybe that person deserved to die."

"Or maybe the person was a victim of me having a bad day."

"That too."

"I don't think anyone saw me."

"Do you need me to do anything?"

Her eyes glossed as she shook her head. I watched to see if a tear would fall, but it didn't. "You're in love. Aren't you?"

"I am."

"The plug?"

"Yes."

"You killed someone the day you and him weren't seeing eye to eye?"

"I did."

I leaned back onto the couch, and suddenly, a thought flashed through my head. Everyone in the crew seemed to have gone soft. "We're all acting like Rel, and I don't like that."

She forced a laugh. "I peeped."

"So, guess what I found out?"

"What?" She rested her head on my shoulder.

"Delyle has a son, and guess who that son is?"

I felt her tense up. "Who?"

"Terry."

"Oh, really? How'd you find that out?"

"Went to the club to see him two weeks ago and saw Terry."

"You went to the club alone?"

"It wasn't during open hours."

"You went to see him alone?"

Tilting my head up and down, I said, "I will explain later."

"What happened?"

"Guess I can explain now. We've had some sexual shit going on."

"Sex? You've been ducking off to fuck him?"

"Not really, but yes."

"I don't have the mental space to figure out what that means."

"I saw Terry, and he told me that was his son. I'm going to use Delyle to see what all I can find out on his son."

"I don't think playing with Delyle again is the smartest thing to do. We can go about this the way we've been doing it."

"And what's that?"

"Let the streets talk to us."

I rolled my eyes and ignored her. "I've found Delyle's weakness."

She sighed. "Oh, God."

"He loves a good pawn, but even a pawn can take down a king if it moves carefully."

ASHA
TOO ANXIOUS TO PLEASE

I'd just dropped Arielle and Bambi off at a house party over on the block we grew up on. Everyone was talking about it, and I decided to let her go to get out of the house. I wouldn't let her get a job, so that was the least I could do. She damn sure wasn't about to be working no traps. All of us agreed on that. I loved the fact that she wasn't a rebellious teenager. It made things that much more simple.

Ever since she'd been at my place, I had learned a lot about her: Though my sister was private, she told her older siblings everything—especially me. She had just told me that she broke it off with the ball player because he wanted her to get married and start a family as soon as the law would allow. She wasn't with it. She had a mind of her own, and I loved that. She had a little bit of all of us in her.

It was a chill Friday, and I was off, so I went to chill with the girls at the trap in North Dallas. Tweety greased Sway's scalp as Sway smoked a blunt. Rel was sitting on the barstool, looking like someone had just stolen a bike from her and sold it. "The hell wrong with you?" I asked Rel.

Sway passed me the blunt. "Another down-low nigga she fucking that's afraid to show her off."

I gave Rel the eye, asking if it was true.

She nodded. "I thought he was different."

"Aahhhhh," we all said in unison. It was always the same story with Rel. It was always about a nigga. Always.

"He was different, y'all. I was so sure of it. He was nice. I even met his mom."

"What nigga?" I asked.

"That nigga Ajax. The one from Florida," Tweety said.

"The head must ain't as good as she thought," Sway said, rolling her eyes.

"I don't know. Maybe I should've tried it on Houston to find out."

Everyone got quiet. Sway blew the smoke out and pointed her finger at Rel with her eyes still on the TV. "You can have that one. And only that one," she warned.

Tweety and I gave each other a confused look, then shrugged. Sway had definitely been on a different type of time lately. Had this been months ago, Rel's head would have been smashed in with a bat by now, no bullshit. Sway had been very open with us about the fact that Delyle kidnapped her and taught her things instead of torturing her. But for a know-it-all like Sway, teaching her something seemed to be bad, too. Not until his case, though. She'd been changing more and more every day. I began to wonder if she was for real or if it was all a front.

I'd also opened up more about Demaris and me. Not that the girls cared, but only the ones close to me knew. I ain't trust nobody else, really. That's why it didn't surprise me when his name came up.

"I saw Demaris at Big T yesterday," Tweet said.

"What was he doing there?" I asked. "Fuck that. What were *you* doing there?" Big T was a legendary place in Oakcliff. It's where you could get all the designer knock-offs, nails done, shoes, cologne, pictures taken, and more. They also had the best pizza and barbecues from time to time. All the mix tapes would drop there first. As a teen, Big T was the place to be.

"I was getting my nails done."

"You know we got heat in the streets. You were a sitting duck up there. Is you cool?" Sway asked.

"I had my pretty bitch." That was her nickname for her gun.

"Them long ass nails. How were you going to shoot?" Rel asked.

She clicked her nails together. "I can work these mothafuckin' nails. Know that."

"Don't do that no more," I told her.

"It was an emergency."

The oven went off, letting me know the chocolate cake I had in there had finished. As I was taking it out with a mitten, the front door came flying open. Before I could grab my gun from the small of my back, Sway, Tweet, and Rel had their guns loaded and pointed at the front door.

"Damn, my bad." Dezz closed the door behind her and walked in front of the TV.

Dezz was still fairly new, only being with us for a little under a year. She was periodically homeless, so besides working at the trap in South Dallas, she also lived there. Though she was only twenty-one, like most of the Spindarellaz, she'd been through more than a little bit. She fell for us pretty quickly and had shown her loyalty many times. With her beautiful brown complexion, natural hips, and fat ass, we used her as bait for a lot of niggas. She didn't mind either.

"Get out the way, regarded ass girl," Sway said, trying to position herself to see around Dezz's fat ass.

"Where Spin at?" Dezz asked, looking around.

"Not here. Now move, damn."

"I was in Ft Worth today with this dude I be fucking on, and he gets a phone call," Dezz said.

I just knew this wasn't about to be good. This was bad. This was really bad.

"Okay?" Sway asked.

"The nigga I be fucking on is the brother of Loc's baby mama."

"Who the fuck is Loc?" Tweety asked.

"Terry's blood brother. You know."

That had Sway's attention. I wanted so badly to tell Dezz's ass kissing behind to get out and don't let the door hit her, but she was too far into the mess. "Well, the bitch was on the phone confused because she said she was at the hospital with Loc and saw Spin sitting right next to Terry and comforting him."

Sway was at a loss for words. "You mean, like close?"

Dezz nodded. "She said they were really close. Almost like they were fucking."

Sway blew her off. "Girl, move. Spin would never."

Dezz grinned like The Joker and snatched her phone from her bra. "I knew you would say that. That's why I got proof." She tossed Sway the phone.

Rel hopped her nosey ass up to see. She and Tweet were all down Sway's neck. I didn't need to see the picture up close to know that it was true. Everything Dezz said was pure facts, and I hated it. This was the beginning of something terrible; I felt it.

The look of satisfaction on Dezz's face sickened me. What was her motive? Why was she so eager to rat on Spin? I had to be missing something.

Sway put the phone to the side, and nothing else was heard coming from her lips. Rel and Tweet decided to stay out of it, but I had something to say.

"Have you talked to Spin?" I asked Dezz.

She bent her lip. "Fuck that bitch if she creeping with the opps."

"Watch your mouth," I said.

"Yeah, be cool and chill," Tweet backed me up.

Rel pussy ass sat quietly, and Sway didn't say anything.

She shrugged. "I'm just saying. We were supposed to drill his ass, and last I recall, she was the one who was so crazy about calling it off."

"I mean, we don't know if he even killed Houston," Tweet said.

Since she said it first, I hopped in. "Exactly."

"So, it's cool to even consider a nigga who is rumored to have killed your brother?" Sway finally spoke up.

Rel shook her head. She was Sway's bitch and agreed with any and everything she said, even if it was wrong.

"It's also not cool to accuse someone who may well have had zero to do with it," Tweet said.

I had to land the blow. "And I know you ain't sitting over there judging. Spin told me you said Terry was Delyle's son. You're fucking the *father* of the man who was said to have killed your man."

Sway ashed the blunt and stood up. Once I saw her removing her earrings, I slid mine off too. Tweet and Rel hurriedly got between us. All the while, Dezz was just grinning. It was something to her.

Just as we were about to start throwing hands around Tweet and Rel, Spin walked through the door. She immediately knew something was wrong. Once she peeped the smirk on Dezz's face, and the mean looks Sway was giving her, she directed her attention to me.

"What's this?"

I pointed at Dezz. "This bitch come in here telling Sway she got proof of you sitting with Terry at a hospital," I said.

"I saw it with my own eyes! The picture is real," Swag said. "You lied to me. I asked you what was wrong on the couch, and you sat there and lied."

As Sway and Spin went back and forth, saying what Dezz had just revealed, I peeped Dezz. She was genuinely satisfied with the mess she caused. "Wait," I said. Everyone shut up. "What are *you* doing fucking with the *other* side?"

She wasn't smiling now. "Yeah," Spin said. "So you fucking with Loc's baby mama's brother? That's what Sway just said, right? You just as guilty as me."

"First of all, I was trying to work my way close to see what I could find out."

"Cap," I said.

"Bitch, so why you just now telling us when you trying to rat on me? That was supposed to be something you told us off the rip."

"We literally *just started fucking*."

Spin had now redirected her attention to Dezz and was ready to haul off on her, but Sway stepped in front of Dezz.

What the fuck?

Spin looked so hurt. "Oh, yeah? That's how it is, Sway?"

"That's who supplies our drugs, huh?" Sway asked.

"Yeah, and so what? We don't barely pay shit, and we getting money," I said, now standing in front of Spin. Sway had another thing coming if she thought I would let her and this bitch jump Spin. "You acting fucking weird," I added.

"To be fair, we never asked for those discounts," Rel said, standing on the side of Dezz and Sway. She'd chosen a side.

"It doesn't matter if we asked or not. All of us are making more than we ever have. We out hustling the niggas. And not to mention the fact that Sway is fucking the mam's father. So, who's really wrong?" Tweet stood beside Spin and me; she'd chosen our side.

Sway peeped what was going on, and an eerie look of calm came over her face. "I'm going to *keep* fucking Delyle until I find out the truth, and once I do, Terry is dead. I don't give a fuck if he's your man. Take it how you want. I'm with whatever," Sway said before grabbing her keys and leaving.

Dezz left with her, but Rel stayed behind.

We all stood there in silence, trying to figure out what the fuck had just happened. Spin was breathing hard and gently pulling her weave out of her face. She looked as if she wanted to spazz out.

"And this bitch just staying to get some cake," Tweet said, referring to Rel.

Ignoring Tweet, I glanced at a distraught Spin. I knew all she was dealing with and felt so sorry for her. This was something she didn't need. "Spin?" Tweet nudged her shoulder.

She snapped out of it. "Yo?"

"You good?"

"Oh yeah, I'm straight." She grabbed her keys and stormed out.

We all looked at each other confused. "You got a pair of balls, and you need to act like it," I said to Rel. "Call me later. I need some fresh air," I said to Tweet and left behind Spin.

"Big for nothing ass nigga," Tweet said to Rel as I was walking out.

"Spin, wait up." I jogged after her before she reached the car. She slid inside, and I got in the passenger seat of her whip.

"I can't believe this shit."

"They were going to find out anyway. It's better this way."

I knew Spin hated disappointing Sway, and Sway hated disappointing Spin. They felt like they owed each other the world. "Fucking Dezz."

"It's something about that bitch that I don't like. No lie. It's like she had all this planned. I might be tripping."

"I peeped," Spin said. She looked straight ahead. "I'm scared, Asha."

"Of what?" This was the very first time I'd seen fear like she had right now.

"I think he's going to find out I did it."

"Who? Terry?"

"It's not Terry I'm worried about."

"Delyle."

"He's going to make it hurt. Terry is the man he's going to send to kill me. I can feel it."

"It won't come down to that. Let's hope it won't. But if it does, we all got your back. Even Sway. We have so many advantages right now."

Demaris was on my mind. Somebody would know if he

found out it was Spin, and they would tell us. We would have some time to prepare.

"He lurked in the background for years, and nobody knew. He's going to kill me, and he knows how."

"Nonsense."

She looked up at me through the middle rearview mirror. "If you're ever put in a position to choose me or you, choose you. Arielle isn't going to stand a chance without you here."

I got out of the car. "Nothing is going to happen to you. I love you. Call me when you get home."

I couldn't let her see me panic. When I got in the car, I lost it and called Demaris. He said to meet him at the old strip club in East Dallas but to leave my phone at home. That's where he was on his way to.

Doing what I was told, I went home to drop off my phone and headed over to the old, empty building. Nobody hardly ever came over there anymore unless it was to do something sinister or sneak off for sex. He could've come to my house, so I knew it wasn't that.

Once there, I parked in the alley and saw a small fire burning. It smelled of charcoal and lighter fluid. The other smell, I couldn't quite make out.

Demaris leaned against the brick wall as he watched the fire burn. I knew he noticed it was me because I was alive and had no bullets flying my way, but he didn't look at me. He had on all black, so something told me he didn't choose right now to throw a barbecue for him and me.

He reached out and pulled me in front of him, cuddling me from behind. "Glad to see you." He leaned down and kissed my neck.

"What's going on?"

"Just handling something." He kissed me again. "I need you to promise me something."

"Anything."

"Don't ever cheat on me."

"Why? You threatening me?"

"No. Just don't ever do it."

"I promise."

"I won't leave you. I think you should know that. But I won't live on this earth with you here and being with another nigga."

"So, if you can't have me, nobody can. Right?" Demaris had started to grow on me more and more. I had never in life had someone feel this strongly about me as he did. It felt so good. It felt dangerous but good.

"Correct."

I shook my head. "You got it, big dawg. But what's on your mind? What got you even thinking like that?"

"I don't feel like nobody should be loving you but me. Not even fool ass."

"Your brother?"

"Yeah, him."

"I would never in life fuck with him again. Then that shit he pulled with my sister at the dinner table. I could just strangle him. I hate him."

"He ain't gon' fuck with her. Believe me."

"I do."

"I want a family."

"Why?" I asked.

"With you."

"I got Arielle. I'm straight," I joked. He wasn't joking.

He kissed me again. "I love you."

"Love you too. What's burning? Some bloody clothes?"

"Nah. My godfather lost his temper today with someone, and I cleaned the body."

"That's a body I smell?"

"Burning flesh."

I almost threw up but held it in. "Who was it?"

"The man who ran over Icis."

"Who's Icis?" I acted as if I didn't know because I wasn't supposed to.

"His first love. Mother of most of his children."

"What happened?"

"She was run over and will be dead once she's removed from life support."

"So, that's who did it?"

"Yeah, but he only ran her over. Someone tossed her into oncoming traffic. He found that out right before he killed him."

I tried to silently swallow the lump in my throat. "So, why kill the man?"

"I told you, he lost his temper."

I had a feeling in my gut that this wouldn't end well. None of it.

Spin
Decisions

The next morning, I was up bright and early, grabbing my things from the loft Sway and I shared. She stood there with a grin on her face as she ate a popsicle, watching me pack.

"I don't need you hovering over me," I told her as I slammed some socks into the suitcase.

"I just don't understand why you're leaving."

"To keep from us getting into it."

"All because I'm going to kill Terry?"

I stopped packing and turned to her. "You're not killing him because he didn't kill Houston."

"Did he tell you this while he was fucking you?" she said, being sarcastic.

Something randomly crossed my mind. "Where is Fray?"

"I don't know. Working." She was lying.

"I pray you didn't do anything to him. Remember what the judge said."

I always told Sway we should record what he did to her, but she was always afraid that he would turn it on her and say it was consensual sex. I told her that it was no way a judge could say that was consensual, but she never did. I think she just didn't want to deal with the theatrics of it all.

"So, just keep letting him rape me? You just hate me."

"No, I told you what we should do. You didn't want that option."

"He's not dead. Relax. Just know he's taken care of."

"You ever stop to think that maybe you shouldn't be fucking the man whose son you want to drill?"

"I could say the same about you."

"What?"

"I read between the lines, Spin. You're the reason Terry's mother is in the hospital. How will he feel?"

"Why is everything a competitive issue with you? I honestly want you to use your brain in this situation."

"Bitch, shut the fuck up. You're making zero sense."

"Then you bucked on me for this bitch Dezz last night. Are you crazy?"

"She had the balls to tell me some shit you didn't have the balls to tell me. You love him? Don't you?"

"I do. So what?"

"How cute. Coming from someone who attended the funeral of a man she loved, wearing something other than black. It will help you not to cry so much. I saw an article about the importance of colors."

"Good to know. Too bad I won't need that information."

"You're choosing him over me?"

"No, Sway. Fuck. All I'm saying is you won't even give him a fair chance."

"He killed your brother, and when it's revealed, you just need to apologize to me."

"For what?"

"For being a dick sprung whore for the opps."

I shook my head. "He's not no *opp*. Sway, they don't even take us seriously. He's annoyed with you, not mad with you."

"Same thing."

"No, it's not. Damn." I took a deep breath. "If you just give him half a chance, you would maybe like him. I mean, you like the man who made him. Are *you* in love?"

"I have an agenda to follow through on."

"Good luck with that." I closed the second suitcase and zipped it. "I'll be back to get the rest of it."

She stepped to the side and allowed me to walk by. "Going to his house, huh?"

"I am."

"Why?" She was on my heels as I walked out.

"Because I need to make sure I'm in the loop if and when they find out about my role in the death of his mother."

"That's not a good idea. I mean, I will move out, and you can stay here. Just don't go there." She was no longer petty. She actually looked afraid for me.

"Don't worry, I'll be fine. I needed this to happen to get ahead of things. I made a huge mistake, and I just need to make this right if I can."

She grabbed my hand. "Look, bitch, he killed your brother. I feel it. So, I call it even. You know? Fuck him."

"Sway, stop. Okay? Just stop. He didn't do anything to me. I just ruined this mama's life, and I need to fix it."

"Tell me how you're going to fix it. If anything, it's going to piss him off that you're there, knowing you killed his mother. Just don't go."

I snatched away from her. "I'll check in every day, but I'm doing this."

She stood there looking defeated. I could tell she really cared, but I also knew she wanted him dead.

I left and headed over to Terry's with no warning call. I didn't tell her this, but I really wanted to be around him because of our last argument. He hadn't said much to me, and I was not about to let Crystal win my man back. She was in the perfect situation to do so while he was vulnerable. I couldn't let that happen. Enough time had passed.

When I first pulled up to his apartment, I didn't see his car outside, but I did see his window open and him looking down at me. He didn't seem too excited. I'm fact, once we locked eyes, he closed the blinds.

All by myself, I hauled my two suitcases up to his place. The door was already open. Diamond lay on the couch with her tongue out, not really bothered by my presence either.

Out of nowhere, Terry appeared in front of me. "What's this?"

"Sway kicked me out. She found out about us," I half lied.

He effortlessly grabbed the heavy suitcases and carried them to the back. I closed the door behind me and locked it. Of course, I searched for any clues that bitch had been there.

"Where's your car?"

"Crystal is using it. Her car is in the shop. They can't figure out what's wrong."

I held my tongue to keep arguments down, but I had to know. "Y'all back at it?"

"Nah, just being a good friend to her like she's one to me."

I left it there. He'd started putting my clothes in the drawers, so that was my answer to a lot of things. "That's nice."

"I've been missing you. It's been two weeks," he said.

"I know. Just wanted to give you space to figure out what you needed to figure out. How's your mom?"

"Still on life support. My dad won't let go. He has this belief that if we give her body time, she will heal. He said he will pull the plug when he's ready."

"Who has rights over her?"

"He does."

"Why?"

"She gave them to him in case of a situation like this. She always said he made the best decisions, and she'd rather him make hers if she couldn't." He paused. "It's like she always knew a time like this would come."

"I'm so sorry." I held him so tightly from behind, resting my head on his back.

"It's all good. I should be apologizing to you, ma."

"Welcoming me back is your apology, and I so gratefully accept."

He forced a laugh. It was almost like laughing was hard for him. "You smell nice."

"Body wash."

"Have you had sex?"

"No, baby."

"Been saving that pussy for me?"

"I have."

"Tell me anything."

"Terry?"

"Yeah."

"What makes you love me?" I felt him tense up. He stopped putting the clothes up and everything.

He then turned to me and picked me up. "What makes you love me?"

"I can't begin to explain. You have this *thing* about you, and it has this tight hold on me."

"You sure it's not just this dick?"

"It's that, too."

"You want it?" he asked.

Just as I was about to answer him, there was a knock at the door. He put me down and went to answer. I followed.

It was Crystal. *Why does this bitch always pop up when I'm here?*

She was grinning until she saw me behind Terry. She then frowned and pried keys from her pocket. "My car is done. Can you take me to get it?"

"Bet." He grabbed his shoes and walked to the back, probably to get his gun. He was never caught without it.

When I was sure he wasn't near, I said to her, "You think you slick?"

"Excuse me?"

"You can't have him. He's mine."

She rolled her eyes as if she was truly exhausted and annoyed. "Listen, I'm just here to get my car, and I need him to take me."

"Okay, bitch, so Uber there."

"Why waste money when he can take me? Please stop talking to me."

Terry came back to the door. "You coming?" he asked me.

"Yeah. Let me grab my shoes and purse."

"We'll be in the car. Lock the door," he said as he followed Crystal down the long stairway.

I hurried up and grabbed my things, then rushed down the stairs. I didn't need them having any alone time. He was already being too nice to her. Too nice for my liking.

Once at the car, I made sure to get by the front door, so she didn't try anything stupid. She rolled her eyes again and got into the back seat.

Bitch.

"You ate yet?" Terry asked once we left the apartment.

"Who?" I wanted to know.

"Both of you."

"Not really. You can get me some Waffle House to go," she said from the back seat.

"What about you?" he asked me.

"Sure. I'll take Waffle House."

"Cool. I'll use this time to talk to my brothers in person about a family matter."

"Your mother?" I asked.

"Yeah. We need someone to try and talk sense into my dad."

"About what?" Crystal asked.

I mugged her so hard. Because why was she asking my man questions like he was still her man?

"He needs to let Mom go sooner than later. She's in pain, and the longer she's alive, the more he prolongs it. He's not thinking about that."

"Yeah, he really needs to let her go."

"I think I have the perfect person to talk sense into him. She might not like it, but it's worth a try."

"Who? Don't tell me, Sway," he said.

"Exactly her."

"Thanks, but no thanks. You goofy."

"You have no idea how she might be able to help."

"That lil' pussy ain't gon' make my dad change his mind. Trust me. It might piss him off. She's better off persuading his wife, and then his wife can make him do it."

"Well, that's an option we can explore."

"We're going to use my older brother. If that doesn't work, we can try it that way."

I grinned, feeling accomplished. "Let's do that." Then a memory of his mom's face right before she was hit by a car struck me like lightning. Damn. Reality set back in so fast.

"Are you ready to let her go?" Crystal asked.

That question must have been hard for him to answer because he hesitated. "I don't think I'm ever going to be ready. I think she was ready."

"Damn. Didn't look at it like that," Crystal said.

Her deep concern for him was truly irritating as hell. It's like he didn't see what she was doing, but I saw it. She was trying her hardest to show she cared more than me.

I rubbed his back. "Everything will work out fine, baby."

"I hope so."

We pulled in front of the Waffle House. Terry walked to two cars on the side as Crystal and I went inside to wait for our carry-out.

I sat at a table in the back, and she came over and sat across from me. She had a different look in her eyes this time. It's like she was revealing to me a secret with her eyes. "You seem nervous. A bit too anxious. Everything okay?"

"Yeah, bitch. Now get before I beat your ass. I've been sparing you."

She chuckled. "You've been sparing me? You really think that, huh?"

"I can show you."

Crystal leaned back and pulled out her phone. She then handed it to me. I looked at her like she was crazy. "Take it."

"Why?"

"Just look at the video."

I took the phone, and in black and white, I saw my car toss Icis into traffic. It seemed to have come from a camera from the house in front of the stop sign where it occurred. I slid it back.

"How did you get this?"

"From my neighbor, right before he left to take it to the police."

"Did he take it to them?"

"No. He didn't."

"Why?"

"Because I spared you. I need you to listen to me."

To Be Continued

Follow Kia Jones

Follow Kia Jones on social media to keep up with the latest:
IG: LoraineLavelle

Also by Kia Jones

When I Needed You The Most

To Be Honest

To Be Honest 2

To Be Honest 3

Made in the USA
Coppell, TX
03 May 2025

48987589R00142